MW01171822

Darkness Unfolds:

The Return of Merlin

"If I do

not stop

the

darkness

then who

will?"

-Merlin

Book 3

By: A.P. Whitfield

To my Nannie and Pawpa who had a love story for the books and knew only

unconditional love. I love you both more than I can ever express. I miss you

Pawpa and not a day goes by that I do not think about you.

A.P.

TRIGGER WARNING
This book contains situations and scenes that may cause people to become triggered. These include but are not limited to: sexual assault, rape, drugs, drinking, blood, gore, murder, and abuse.

Chapter 1

The moon hung high in the night sky with stars that dusted the navy blue to black that coated the evening. Pulling my motorbike to a stop next to a sidewalk to take a break, I pulled my helmet off to shake out my hair before running my fingers through it. I was only planning on passing through to get to my next destination and my bike needed gas. From this stop I got an odd feeling that this town was not normal. Something was off about it. Furrowing my brows together I looked up and down the almost deserted road in the town. Catching my eye across the street I spotted a bed and breakfast that held a Victorian style to it. Dismounting the bike, I grabbed my rucksack, threw it over my shoulder and grabbed the other bag to make my way across the street. I had my leather jacket zipped up as the evening air cut through me but even in that chill, I could feel something was not quite right with the town I had stopped in.

Finding the dining room still open, I slipped in hearing the bells give a ring. I let my eyes wonder over the interior of the place that looked like time had stood still from the furniture to the crown molding. Removing my rucksack, I sat at the table closest to a burning fire in an old large wood burning fireplace. Taking notice, it was not a busy night but then again, I was coming through rather late. Taking the menu that was on the table I read through what was listed. A slight scowl crossed my supple lips as I let out a sigh and rolled my eyes. I was starting to grow tired of quick foods but at least it seemed like they had more homemade meals to pick from, it was a bed and breakfast after all. I had been on the road for far too long and it was wearing on me. Playing with my ring that was made of two dragons encircling two amethyst crystals I let my mind start to wonder. Rubbing my tired eyes, I rested my elbows on the table. I was going to hope they had hot teas. I was not one for coffee, but it seemed rather unlikely. Then there was the problem of finding a place to bunk for the night if they did not have any open rooms at this bed and breakfast.

"You're not out of the woods yet Daniel." I said to myself. At least that was the name I was going by now. The less people knew about me the better and the less people I got attach to the better. At least that is what I told myself.

Rubbing my hand on my face I sighed heavily and looked back at the menu then pushed it away and waited for someone to serve me but out of habit I

8

kept messing with my ring or necklace. It was a nervous habit of mine. Keeping the same tired but serious gaze I let my eyes take in the building and studied the customers in it. I could feel magick in the air and not the romantic kind. It was a mix of dark and light and it seemed as if both were fighting to outweigh the other.

"I really do need to get out of this town." I whispered to myself. "Wouldn't you agree Amethyst?" A little snout poked out of my rucksack, and I pressed my index finger to my lips as if to hush the little purple dragon that looked up at me with big green eyes. Smiling down at my companion I chuckled softly. "I'll get you food boy but for now you have to stay hidden. If anything, I'll get it To-Go so we can find a room if they do not have one here and then I can feed you…. Now don't give me that look." I scowled as I talked in hushed tones to Amethyst. It was always like this with the two of us. Amethyst could grow in size and would normally be in my ring resting but he insisted on riding with me out of the ring where he resided. "You would think after almost three centuries you would be nicer to me." I grumbled and gave Amethyst a side glance that was only greeted with a smile. Shaking my head, I poked Amethyst back into my rucksack before he was seen.

"Sorry about your wait sweetheart. What can I get for you tonight?" The young woman asked and seemed to take a keen interest in me, or so it seemed, "You're not from around here are you?" She questioned.

I pierced my lips together and raised a brow. "No. I am not." I gave a short reply without giving her much of a look.

A slight pout rested on her lips at my ability to ignore her looks.

"I'd like to place my order To-Go if you will. I'll have one cheeseburger with a side of chips… fries. Sorry you lot call them fries here…. And I'll also take your grilled shrimp skewers and a side salad. No dressing. Oh, and a hot cup of black tea. I will need the milk for it on the side." I instructed. "Definitely not from around here." She jotted everything down taking note of my accent and that seemed to only make her more interested. "I- I will get this right out for you. Would you like a cup of tea while you wait for your food to be prepped to take home?"

I frowned at the words "*home*," licking my lips I gave her a half smile. "That would be lovely. Thank you."She nods to me and leaves me alone to go turn in my order.

Home.

A word I was not familiar with. *'At least not since…yes… then.'* I said to myself in my mind. The clinking of a cup and saucer was sat in front of me with a side of milk. Looking up at the young woman that gave me a worried look that I only returned with a polite smile and nod, "thank you ma'am."

"Are you okay?" She asked me.
"Yes, no need to fret. Thank you for your concern." I replied to her, "where is your closest place for lodging for the night or do you happen to have something available on short notice here?" I inquired.

"Oh here, just up those stairs are the rooms you can rent from the owner of this bed and breakfast. I can help get you set up. How many nights will you be staying?" She perked up as she watched me.
I went about adding the white sugar first and then the milk after, "only for tonight." I stirred in the mix without looking back at her but by the sound of the sigh that left her lips I could tell she was disappointed.
"Hopefully you'll change your mind by morning, but I will go talk to the owner and get you a room key. I can show you up after your food comes out." The waitress looked back down at me with sad eyes before walking away with a pout.

I leaned back more in my seat and closed my eyes for a moment to think. The warmth from the teacup I had my hands wrapped around warmed me up slightly. *"365 days. That is how long I have been…"* I did not finish my thought. It pained me too much to do that. My chest tightened and a flash of her face crossed my memory. No matter how hard I wanted to forget her, I couldn't. Her laughter echoed in my mind with flashes of her blue eyes that seemed to smile at me. *"God how I missed her."* Reluctantly I brought the hot liquid to my lips and took a sip of it. It wasn't as good as what they had back in Europe, but that was to be expected. I had been in the states long enough to know that and lived many lives to learn it as well. It would never measure up to a cup of proper English tea or what they had in Italy at least.

"You seem troubled. Care to let an old timer join you and talk on your troubles? I've lived long enough to know a thing or two about life."
Looking up I locked eyes with a pair of old gray ones belonging to an elderly man who was smiling down at me. He had a head full of white hair and a gentle look about him. "Yes, of course." I replied to him returning his smile with a tired one of my own.
"I know that look all too well." He said to me as he took a seat across from me. "Name is Jud." He stuck out his hand for me to shake and I politely took it. His hand was rough and showed he spent time doing hard labor. The thick calluses brushed against my own as he gave my hand a firm shake. "My wife owns this place."
"Daniel." I replied and took another look over the place. "It's a nice bed and breakfast." I avoided the other topic but of course he went back to it.
"You're missin' a girl aren't cha." Jud had a southern accent as he spoke to me. He rubbed the back of his neck and chuckled. I could tell he was about to tell me a story. I avoided reading his thoughts. The story seemed important to him, and I wanted to respect it. "I can tell you it wasn't easy for us. Her family didn' care much for me. I was a poor farm boy that never finished school. I made it to fourth grade and had to quit to help work the fields. I worked the very fields her family owned. The rich upper class ya'know, I was even workin' the stables. That's where I was when I first laid eyes on her. I was seventeen. She was sixteen. I never saw someone so beautiful; she had her brown hair pulled back out of her face and fair complexion. Brown eyes that reminded me of root beer. Always dressed neatly like she was out of a Sears Catalog. Still to this day she is the most beautiful woman I have ever seen." Jud chuckled to himself and looked back at me. I glanced down at my cup of tea with a sad smile on my face, he sighed and went on with his story, "at first I didn't catch her attention…"
"You did but I had to play hard to get. I couldn't make it easy for you. I wanted you to work for it." I looked up to see an elderly woman with white hair pulled back come over with my food. She leaned down and kissed his cheek. "Now don't scare him away. You can show this young man where he will be staying for the night. I added a slice of pie to your order. On the house." She gave me a warm smile and a wink.
"Thank you ma'am." I said softly and took the key and bag from her. "What do I-?"
"It was taken care of. You owe nothing." She said to me. I gave her a confused look but nod to her. "I am MaryBell. If you need me for anything, just give me a holler. I hope you enjoy your stay."

I watched her walk away and I looked back at the bag and then to Jud who was chuckling at my expression.

"You act as if you're new to someone showing you kindness." Jud studied me for a moment, and I lowered my eyes to avoid his, but I still caught sight of the frown that rested on his face. "Come. Let's get ya to your room."

I grabbed my stuff only for him to take my other bag from me to take up stairs. "Now where was I? Oh yeah, well I worked at getting her attention. She had many young men that came from high class families that called on her but she never much cared for em'. She would run those poor saps off." He chuckled and shook his head. "Her parents were so mad at how she behaved. A wild child they would call her. But I thought she was perfect, kept me on my toes every time she came around."

We walked up the stairs and reached the floor for the lodging. I followed him down the hall to another flight of stairs to the next floor. The area was decorated in a beautiful Victorian style that matched the look of the home. It was like stepping into a time capsule.

"Till one day she came into the barn I was working in takin' care of the horses. I remember her looking right at me and she said, *"farm boy. I need a date for tonight's showdown at the country club and I want you to take me"* I was shocked, but I gave her a nod and said, *"yes ma'am"* I could not for the life of me understand why she wanted me to be the one to take her, but I did. Needless to say, I felt out of place and the looks I got weren't much better. I knew what they all thought of me. I was a poor farm boy that would never get anywhere and I wasn' smart enough to do anything else but plow the fields and take care of animals. After that night we was always together. She snuck around to see me. One day turned into another and into another and we was always sneakin' off together." He gave me a wink at the last part, and I chuckled at the old man. "Look, he can smile and laugh." He patted my shoulder and unlocked the door to my room, "well, I best let you get settled. I'm sure you're tired of hearin' me talk."

"No… can you stay? I would like to hear the rest." I didn't know why I wanted to hear it. I guess I was also feeling a bit lonely. Jud was kind and I missed the presence of another.

Jud looked back at me and frowned as I looked away and sat the food on the little table and my bag on the bed. "Of course son." He said gently. I licked my lips and felt my chest tighten as I took a seat. "That was a summer I would never forget. It was the start of our relationship. Her parents found out. At first, they just thought what we had was a rebellious faze their daughter was going through and would come out of it. Spring turned into

12

Summer, Summer turned into autumn and we wasn' breaking up. I pulled up the drive one night after coming home from the drive-in in my old pickup. It was a Chevy, still got it, I restored it, beautiful cherry red. Anyways, I was greeted at the door with a not so happy Pa. He took me inside into another room, I could hear MaryBell yellin' at her ma. I was being called trash, no good, filth. All of that. Labeled out to be no good and going nowhere. Then her father spoke, he was calm. He handed me a check. He wanted to pay me off and stay away from his daughter, I wouldn't take it or do it. That night we both decided to run away and get married. So, we did. The next week. June 27, 1959· we got married under a crying tree… you know those trees they call sad but look beautiful."

"A Weeping Willow?" I questioned with a chuckle.

"That's it. Weeping Willow. We went to the town over and got hitched by a pastor. He was even in flip-flops." Jud chuckled and let the toothpick in his mouth roll around as he spoke. I had yet to notice he was rather tall, probably about 6'0 and had a bit of a round belly. His smile was one that could make anyone do the same. He had a kindness about him that felt like home. They both did. "But August 1964, I was sent to Nam."

Sipping on my tea I looked at him and watched his eyes sadden over. I remembered Vietnam, I was there. It was hell.

"You look like a man that was in my unit." Jud finally said. "Smart man. Very clever and quick. The best with a gun than most of us." I stopped and looked back at him and studied him more. His eyes locked on mine and his eyes lingered over to my ring and necklace. "Just like him… it must be lonely never aging and out living everyone. What a dreadful life to live."

"How long have you known it was me, Judson?" I asked and looked back at my tea.

Chapter 2

"As soon as I saw you. There was no doubt about it. I even knew in Nam there was something different about you. A lot of the men didn' care for you but I liked ya. You was smart and brave. You took the risk none of us would do. I guess it was because you knew you couldn' die so you did it to try and save us as much as you could." Jud replied to me and leaned forward on the table to study me more. "Now tell me your story old man." He chuckled.

I half laughed and leaned back on my seat shaking my head, "for all of them calling you an idiot, you are not that Jud."

"You even still write me back. So, you go by Daniel now? Why change the name? Elijah was nice." Jud questioned me.

I shrugged, "I had to change it as time went on along." I sighed as I watched him nod his head in understanding. "Thank you for always writing back. I enjoy the letters and post cards. Even the pictures of your family. Your children now have children of their own. Some even have kids that are married with children of their own." I pulled out my wallet to retrieve the recent pictures I had of the grandchildren and the great grandchildren.

"They are lovely Jud." He looked at the pictures with a little smile on his face.

"So, this is why you stopped comin' around after so long. You don't age. We missed havin' you for the holidays. The kids always loved you. You was good with them." Jud slid the pictures back to me and I tucked them safely away back into my wallet. "Tell me your story old man."

I shifted in my seat and swallowed hard. Judson was an old friend. One I stay in contact with. I had not seen him in so long, but I saw plenty of his family from the little wallet sized pictures that he would send. From time to time I used to get one of them but then those Christmas cards turned into those of his grandchildren with the pets. I still enjoyed them and saved them. I tried to keep my same PO box so it was never too hard to find me and if I did move I always wrote to him to inform him of the address change but I did try to limit doing that. Looking back at him I frowned and licked my lips, "it is easier if I show you…"

"Show me?" Jud questioned in slight confusion.

14

"Yes." I let out a shaky breath and lifted my hand and with a flick of the wrist, *"memoriapraet."* Those words rolled smoothly off my tongue and the room went dark only to show images over a single vacant illuminated wall. My past came flooding back in flashes telling the story of whom I was. "You are right. I am an old man." I chuckled dryly. "I was partly raised in a village that ran along the borders of Camelot. The village was called Jade. It was a mining village for the most part. My father was of course a miner…" I glanced over at Jud who was looking at the images in shock. Hesitating I went on with the story. "I was born into a lower-class family. They gave me the name Merlin." He snapped his head around to look at me with his eyes wide then back at the projected past memories. "Ever since I was small, I was… I was what you can call magically gifted. They did not like that and tried to get me to stop and would pray over me because they thought I was born with the devil in me, being what I was and being able to do what I could do. They feared me even though I tried to make their life easier…. On my 12th birthday I was dragged out of the home I shared with my parents that sat off in the woods. I was confused and scared… they tied me to a stake then set fire to it. I screamed and cried till my throat was bleeding, I told them I would be good. I would listen. That I was sorry." I watched him cover his mouth as tears streamed down his face at what he was seeing. I muted out the screams so I wouldn't wake others that were in the rooms around mine. "They packed their things and left, left me to burn to death. Somehow, I was able to use my own powers to get free… My body started to heal itself quickly. I laid on the ground my melted clothes sticking to my burnt flesh that was healing. I remember the look my parents gave me. They looked at me with such hate…" Wetting my lips I let out another shaky breath. "Weeks went past, and my parents never came back for me. Everyone in the village feared and hated me, wanted me dead. I started to steal food just to be able to eat but it became harder and harder. I had yet to learn completely what I could do. I did not understand what I was and still to this day I have no idea where my powers came from. I was lonely, so lonely that somehow out of that loneliness I created a companion, this little guy. Amethyst, this is Jud, Jud, this is Amethyst." Jud jumped at the sight of the dragon that hopped out of the rucksack wagging his tail with his tongue out like an excited puppy. He nudged my hand, and I knew he wanted his food, so I stopped for a moment to lay his burger and chips down for him to enjoy. "So needy." I shook my head and looked at Jud who was still trying to understand everything. He was a mix of emotions. "I can stop if you wish." I said to him quietly.

"No. Tell me more. I want to understand what brings you here now. What happened with you." Jud said to me and looked back at the paused image of a little boy shivering in the snow suffering from starvation and the cold.

"My mentor found me and took me in. He fed and clothed me. Gave me another chance at life and helped me learn more about myself. He was amazed at what I could do. He said I was not a normal wizard, to be careful and that many would fear me. He was right. Time went on and he took me to live in Camelot. That is when I encountered Morgana. She was so beautiful, so kind and gentle. I never understood the stories they have now portraying her as evil and my enemy. She was far from that. I did not know it on this day, but she would become the most important person in my life and also the love of my life. I was only 13 but I knew as soon as I saw her that I was captivated by her. She did not care what my social status was nor did Arthur. I grew close to the siblings. I lived in the palace and became the royal wizard to the crown but to fool the Vatican and church, I was labeled the royal healer. I grew stronger in my abilities, and I went to any lengths to ensure that I was just that. Regardless of my power I still was not strong enough to equal the crown. Uther, Morgana's stepfather, did not care for me. He only cared about what I could provide him with. I had a hunch the royal family was that of witches and wizards as well and as I grew more into my powers and abilities, I learned that my hunch was right, and I grew to be able to read minds as well. I studied and studied and worked hard to master every bit of my powers. I would spend a lot of time training with Arthur as well. He and his family never knew that I knew what they were. I never said anything. We would spend hours letting our blades clash together all in good sport and I would beat him constantly unless his father came around then I would let him win. Morgana would come and watch us from time to time I knew she was smitten over me, as was I over her. It got to be around the same time every day we would meet in the woods away from others. We would walk and talk together until one day I took the chance and I kissed her. I was 16 then. After that I took any chance I could get to get kisses from her. In empty corridors, courtyards, stables, the woods. Anywhere." I laughed softly as I felt a soft blush grace my features. I felt his eyes linger over me in amusement. "As I continued to get older, Uther caught wind of mine and hers affair and had me whipped till I was unconscious on more than one occasion. She was to be wed to a man by the name of Lord Thomas. At the time I do not think it had hit Morgana and I that we were in love yet. I had a Lady in Waiting that I also entertained on the side. Her name was Juliette. I had been sleeping with them both you could say. Morgana was my first and I was crazy for her, but it was easier to see Juliette. Juliette would talk to me and tell me things Morgana wouldn't. I could read her mind but out of respect for her I wouldn't. Juliette had informed me about Uther and what she thought he was doing to Morgana. To my horror when I done my own investigation, she was right. I wanted to kill him but if I did and they found out I would have been hanged. I still wasn't sure how my powers of returning to the land of the living worked or if I even could again. I knew I could heal but to come back from the dead was another thing. My hate for Uther grew even more." I investigated my empty teacup and looked back at Jud. "You wouldn't happen to have anything stronger? I believe for the rest of the story we will need it."

Jud blinked a couple of times and gave a nod. "Of course, I will be right back. You should eat. You haven' touched your dinner. You need to eat." He got to his feet to leave my room and go off down the hall.

I looked down at Amethyst who had finished his meal and was curled up at my feet sleeping. Bending down I lifted him up into my arms gently to hold him to me. He nuzzled into my chest, and I couldn't help but smile at my companion. Getting up I walked over to the bed to lay him down and covered him up. "Thank you for always being by my side old friend." I whispered and kissed the top of his head. Going back to where I was sat, I opened the container. I honestly wasn't hungry, but I knew I needed to eat. I took a few bites before Jud came back in and sat a bottle of whisky and two glasses on the table. Popping the top off he poured us both a glass. "Thank you."

He held up the glass and gave me a nod. "You don't seem like a whisky man but it's all I got."

"It will work. I can drink anything." I reassured him. "Where was I… Oh right. Well Juliette had gone missing. We could not find her anywhere. We searched all over but she was nowhere to be found. This had happened when I was gone. I had set out on a mission of my own. When I was leaving Lord Thomas and his sister Lady Ophelia Moriarty had come to court. I had read their minds and knew what they had planned. It was to kill Arthur or Morgana after one of them had wed. The main goal was Arthur. Wed him, bore his child and then kill him by poisoning him. Morgana was just another means to get to the crown and to the power and gold that the royal family brought. I told Arthur what they had planned but before Arthur could send word to Morgana, he was sent off to war. When I had returned it had been several months. Morgana was engaged to Thomas and the wedding was being planned. It was on hold because she had fallen ill. That was why I returned. Word was sent to me that I was needed back at the palace. At first,

I thought it was Thomas who had done it but after reading his mind I was wrong. He was worried and scared for her health. The man had fallen in love with Morgana. Reading more of his thoughts though, I uncovered more dirty secrets regarding him and his sister. She was the one who was trying to kill Morgana. Not for the power and glory of being a royal but because she was jealous of her. Jealous that she was stealing her brother, her lover."

"Her what?! I think my hearing is goin' did you say lover?" Jud wiggled a finger in his ear trying to fix his hearing that wasn't broken.

"No, you heard right. Lover. Her and Thomas were sexually active with one another and she was in love with her brother." I let out a heavy sigh and looked at the images playing out. I was by Morgana's bedside. She was weak and frail. Ophelia was there helping her drink down broth. I couldn't help but glare at the woman who played out like a worried friend to Morgana. Morgana started to cough and weaken more, and I worked frantically to make a potion to cure her. I had yet to master what I can do now. It was a race against time, and I could tell Morgana did not have long. To add to my problem, Ophelia had become somewhat taken with me. She worked to corner me and get me alone. She wanted me to teach her. I kept refusing till she got the king involved. After that I had no choice. I made sure I did not teach her anything of major importance, she was relentless, sneaking into my chambers and requesting me to have sex with her. I never would. Finally, I decided to confront Thomas. In doing that it turned into an argument. I told him I knew everything. I laid out the details of it all. He threatened to out me and my powers and have me burned at the stake. I told him I was going to expose him and his sister if they did not leave court regardless of what would happen to me, that Arthur already knew and he was ready to put an end to them when he got home from war. Thomas in his anger pulled his sword on me and stabbed me through... after he stabbed me, he went to try and finish me off. I found a letter opener on the ground I assumed was from me falling back into the desk and it being knocked off... anyway, I picked it up and I shoved it into his chest... through his heart. He did manage to stab me again... my wounds healed but I was still covered in my own blood and now his. I couldn't believe what I had just done. I had killed a noble. I would hang for it if they found out. It was late at night. I wasn't even meant to be at the castle I was supposed to be in a town over getting things for the wedding that would take place as soon as Morgana was better... but I wasn't. I quickly left the castle and discarded of my bloody clothes and burned them. I put on fresh clothes and made my way back to the other town and let them all believe that I was not on the grounds when the murder of Thomas happened. If anyone had seen me, they didn't

say anything. Anyway time passed and Morgana and I grew even closer, and Uther knew it and I would pay dearly for each passing time because of it. Beaten and tortured to no end because of it. I could have killed him, made it stop but I didn't... God I wanted to. He talked down on me constantly, spat at me, humiliated me and degraded me. A lot of times in front of Morgana. Those were the worst. Her expression to what he would do to me hurt worse and her pleas for me to fight back broke my heart. She knew I could do it, kill them all, bring that damn castle down around us and send those uptight royals up in flames. Arthur never knew just how horrible his degenerate father was. He was sent away a lot, much like Uther would make me go with Arthur on quests leaving Morgana unprotected in the castle. Finally, Morgana had enough... I am not sure what drove her to do it, but I suppose it was a mix of mine and her torment. She asked me to kill Uther and I did not give it another thought. I poisoned him with help of a kitchen boy who wanted his own revenge. He had been whipped the previous week for dropping a dish and breaking it. Oddly enough the chamber maids that were faithful to Morgana caught wind and wanted to help as well. Soon all the servants that had been mistreated by that man wanted to help. I made the potion and passed it on to the kitchen boy and him and the others made sure that they gave Uther a spoon full of the potion in his wine or tea. Soon he started to deteriorate, started to die. Believing he caught the fever Morgana had. Never knowing he was poisoned. I acted as if I was treating him, but I was only giving him more of the poison. When he was taking his last breath, I leaned in and whispered to him, *"Checkmate. I take the king."* He looked up at me with pure horror and shock and tried to cough out for me to be taken but he keeled over. I had a sick satisfaction in watching him suffer and die at my hands. I only wish I had made his death more painful." The coldness in my voice and the darkness that crossed over my face made Jud flinch slightly.

"I assume there is more to this story of yours." Jud questioned after a moment.

"There is, Arthur came into rule. We had stayed on good terms with the kingdom of Prehnite and we aided one another in battle when it was needed. We helped each other in trades as well. Prehnite was ruled by an immortal called Argon and his betrothed Citrine." I went on to explain the two immortals and the other two that served under them and their story and what I knew of them. "Both kingdoms had a common enemy and his name was Areses. He was a ruthless ruler who showed no mercy or kindness to his people or to others unless it would suit him. He crossed the line and started to attack both our kingdoms with the aid of his demonic children, and I say

demonic because they are just that. Born from the pits of hell. It took all of us to seal him away. He was powerful. It wasn't easy but we did do it. It cost us a lot of lives in the process, but his children did retreat. Sometime later I encountered Ophelia again. On less than friendly terms of course. I wasn't aware as to where she had gone or had been those couple of years or what she had been up to. She had been with Areses. He taught her a lot of dark sick tricks. Her and I had a battle in our crossing. She tried to kill me. I was surprised at how strong she had gotten. I was taken aback by it. She wanted revenge. She knew I had killed her brother and I was the reason Areses was gone... but I won... at least I thought I had..."

"You *thought*?" Jud arched a brow at my words as he watched with great interest at what I was showing him.

"Yes. I will get to that, skipping ahead several years, Morgana and I were living happily together. Arthur had given his blessing and we were going to be married that December and to add to our happiness she was pregnant. I was to be a father. I was overjoyed, we both were." I looked at the happy image of Morgana. Her sweet laughter made my heart swell up. "December had come, and we had lived through a plague and war. Arthur wanted to do something to celebrate life, so he had a ball and invited many to join. It was beautiful. I knelt and talked to our baby and kissed her stomach before the ball. She couldn't help but laugh at my ways. I wanted to be a better father than mine was. I wanted to prove I was good... good enough. That night I waltzed with Morgana. She looked so beautiful. She was two months pregnant.... She wasn't showing too much yet, but she still had a glow about her." Letting out a shaky breath I went on with the story. "During the ball Camelot was attacked. I kissed Morgana one last time and I promised her I would return to her and our child. Her and the other women and children were taken to safety. Arthur and I went out to battle. I summoned Amethyst to aid us. We were winning. We had the upper hand until Areses' children showed up and after that things went wrong. They had somehow gotten their hands on a spell of mine involving dark objects and used my own work against me and my dragon. Arthur was forced by his first in command back behind the stone walls for his protection, but he saw all that was happening and tried to force his way to get to me, but they wouldn't let him pass and I told him to stay back. I was taken away... that was the last time I saw any of them. I could hear Morgana screaming for me. I looked back at her pained expression as her personal guards held her back. She had managed to find her way to us... I guess she knew something would go wrong... for months I was tortured. In every single way possible. Repeatedly. All hours of the day or night. They acted as if they wanted information on Arthur, but I knew it was more than that. They wanted revenge on me for what happened to their father. They knew I orchestrated it." I swallowed hard and took large sips of the whisky that burned going down. Jud did the same as he watched the disturbing torture go on. "Then the worst of it happened…" I showed him what had happened to Morgana. I watched as the old man across the small table from me cried at the sight of the young woman's torment up until her death. I showed him everything Clara had showed me two years ago. The next flash of the story went back to me. I was on my knees struggling to stay conscious. Mortem yanked my head back and chuckled in my ear and in a sick voice I remember clearly what he had said, *"No wonder you enjoyed that princess of yours so much. She was a good fuck. Even gorgeous when pregnant, too bad I had to have her head. I thought I'd let her, and your child pay you one last visit."* I wasn't hungry anymore. I could tell Jud was trying not to vomit at the sight of Morgana's head in the basket with my dying son in it. It was a lot to take in. You could see the moment I snapped. I showed Jud everything. I went through the story of each life with him. "Every life I found her, and we have a moment together, but it is one that is always taken from us. I found her again. She goes by Clara now." I showed him what happened leading up to this moment. "She is now wed to the King of Norway. His name is Wesley LayFate. His father was killed going into their senior year at Prospero that led them to wed early. He was murdered by a warlock. I am not sure which one. Nor are they. She now has a son…" I pulled out my phone to show him a picture of Clara with her baby boy who had a head full of blonde curls and big blue eyes hugging a stuffed purple dragon that she named Amethyst after my dragon.

"She is beautiful… so is her boy… I am sorry Elijah… Daniel… what do I call you?" Jud studied the picture and looked back to me who held pain in his eyes. "I am sorry for all you have been through son. I wish I had known all you have been facing on your own. You always have a place with us. You always have."

I gave him a sad smile. "Merlin is just fine… I might as well use my old name. No matter what, the ones who want me are coming for me and I am working to stop them from hurting more people… I did not want to get you involved. I wasn't aware I ended up in Wilmington, North Carolina. I have been a bit out of it and just following leads to reach Ophelia and it led me this way. I knew you lived around here I just did not know where. You and I always used the post office mailboxes. I should have known…. I have been so distracted…"

"And you are missing your girl." Jud cut me off and nods to my phone that held the picture of Clara and her son.

I lower my brow and frown as I looked at her picture and traced her features. "You are a good man, Merlin. You always have been. I may not have known you as long, but I knew when I first met ya on the frontline that you was good. You risked your life for many of us and you stood by the words, *"no man left behind"* you made sure many of us made it back to our loved ones. I believe in you, and I believe if anyone can save us all it's you. I might be an old man, but I ain't leaving you behind to do this on your own and by the looks of the messages popping up on your phone it shows you still have others on ya side as well, even if that Sebastian boy and others aren't right now. You still have Arthur, that girl Jenna, Chester, those immortals and Clara and even your ma now. It weren't your fault that Stella died. Stop blaming yourself for everything that goes wrong." I watched Jud finish his glass and get to his feet. "Now you need to finish eating and then get some sleep. MaryBell I know is waiting for me to come to bed so I best be off so we can get up early and get the bed and breakfast open and stuff. If you need us just holler. We're right down the hall." Patting my shoulder, I watched him take his leave. "G'night Merlin. It's good to have you back with us."

I watched him leave of my room and I looked down at my food. I wasn't hungry but I knew it would be rude if I didn't eat it. I didn't get to thank Jud before he left my room, but I had a feeling he knew I was thankful for them and what they were doing for me. Reluctantly I started to eat again. Looking back at my phone at the text messages and read each of them, all full of worry. Most of them from my mother. Chester of course tried to play off his worry with jokes and the random TikToks he found humorous. Jenna was always texting and calling. We had gotten to where we were working closer together to trying to solve things. I was keeping my word to her. At least I was trying to. Arthur was always blowing up my phone. I knew he was scared to lose me again. Clara would text and call me in secret. It was hard for her, but she managed. I had not heard from her all week until tonight. It was getting harder for her to contact me, and it led to a lot of fighting between her and Wesley. She had called me one night and he found out and it turned into them arguing while she was still on the phone with me. We had been Facetiming at the time, so I heard and saw the arguing. I tried to not get into it with him to not make it worse on Clara, but I lost my temper when I watched him jerk the phone out of her hand and refuse to give it back to her. Since then, she has had to be cautious about talking to me. We had met in secret quite a few times since last year leading up to now. It wasn't easy but Jenna and Chester have helped with it to cover for her. Sad to say it had resulted to that. Mostly Jenna with letting Clara hide out in her home or a hotel she would be in to let us have time together. Of course, Clara would spend time with Jenna after or before, it was never a complete lie and given I could pop in whenever unseen it did make it easier, so she wasn't seen with me. But we were back to being a secret again. Like all the other times before. I hated it.

Chapter 3

I had a restless night of sleep. I had tossed and turned all night with my dreams plagued with nightmares of my past. I woke up in cold sweats panting. Amethyst was looking at me with worried eyes, nuzzling me and gave me a few licks on my face, "down boy… down. I am fine. Just a nightmare is all." I said to him but was only greeted with worried whimpers. I laid back on my pillow and looked up at the ceiling that had beautiful detail crown molding. Closing my eyes again I still could not shake each image that flashed through my mind. Rolling over I grabbed my phone off the nightstand to look at the time and saw I had several missed calls from Jenna and even Chester. Sitting up I pressed her name to call her back. It couldn't be a coincidence that they both were calling me.

"Daniel. Clara is missing and so is the baby." Jenna quickly said after only letting the phone ring one time. My blood ran cold at her words, and I was up out of the bed quickly.

"What happened? When were they last seen?" I asked as I slipped my AirPods in and got dressed.

"I don't know. They were last seen in the palace in her personal chambers." Jenna replied franticly into the phone. I could hear the panic in her voice as I worked to calm my own.

"Where are you now?" I asked her. "Were there clear signs of a struggle? How did her guards not hear anything?" I questioned her more.

"I am at the palace with her family. Chester and his girlfriend are with us… I don't know I guess it happened during guard change… No. No struggle but they could have threatened to kill the baby if she did try anything. Please… we need your help…" She whispered into the phone as if it were her that was the only one making the request and honestly it probably was. Her and Chester.

I went to respond when a knock came to my door. "Merlin? It's Jud. Are you awake son… someone…" Jud didn't have to finish his sentence. I quickly opened the door to let my eyes land on them. On Clara and her son Noah. "Clara…"

"Clara? She is with you?" Jenna whispered loudly into the phone. "Oh, thank the saints." She breathed out but I could hear clear chatter on the other

end and a lot of it was angry. "Oh, will you lot shut the hell up. At least they are safe." Jenna scolded and hung up.

I still couldn't believe it. She was in Wilmington.

"Hello Merlin…" Clara said softly. She had a shy look on her face as she held the small child in her arms.

Jud looked between the two of us. "I will leave you two be for a moment. When you're ready, breakfast is being served."

I was still only half dressed as I finished buttoning up my dress shirt, my eyes not leaving her. "Clara what are you doing here? The whole royal guard is looking for you. Why would you…" she moved close to me, leaned up on her tiptoes and kissed me deeply. I was taken aback for a moment but leaned in and held her close and returned the kiss till I felt little hands patting me. Pulling away slightly I looked down to see the little boy smiling up at me. "It is nice to meet you little one." I let my thumb stroke his soft chubby cheeks and chuckled at him trying to gum on my hand. I looked back into Clara's sad blue eyes and frowned. "What is wrong Clara?" I questioned her sadly.

"I had to see you. I cannot stay a prisoner in that place any longer, always being watched. I hate it. I… I do not wish to go back. Please…" Tears ran down her face as she spoke to me. I gently pulled her into my room and closed the door behind me.

"Clara it isn't safe being with me. You and Noah could get hurt. I do not wish that for you. You could stay with Jenna. You know she can take down that whole army. When she hung up, she was already laying into them."

It pained me to see her this way. I knew she was unhappy. Noah was the only one who had brought her joy in that whole arrangement.

"But you are who and what I want. I don't care about any of what others say I want you and I am so tired of pretending and doing what others want and expect of me." Clara was clearly in distress as I helped her sit down on the bed. Noah crawled out of her arms and over to Amethyst and hugged the dragon tightly and giggled. I assumed he thought it was his plushie. Amethyst didn't seem to mind he only returned the affection with playful licks. Clara let a sad smile sit on her lips as she watched the two. "You are my home. I do not wish to be anywhere else but with you."

"I understand Clara and I want you… more than anything but it is not safe being with me. It could get you both killed if you stay with me." I placed both of my hands on her shoulders gently and looked into her sad blue eyes that held tears. "I love you so much…"

"I love you… I know the risk… I will figure something out but for now please…"

"Clara they will come for you now that they know you are with me and if it isn't them, it will be someone or something connected with Ophelia."

"I know Merlin…" She cupped my cheek and I leaned into her touch that I had long and missed. I kissed the palm of her hand and then leaned in to kiss her forehead.

"Okay, I will do everything I can to keep you safe and with me. Even if it costs me my head." I said gently while I moved her into my lap to hold her in my arms. She rested her head on my chest as silent tears ran down her face soaking into my shirt. We stayed like that for what felt like hours, but it was only a few minutes. I let her cry and gather herself and helped to clean her tears away. I hated seeing her like this. It broke my heart to know she was this unhappy and forced to live a life she did not want.

"I am sorry… You probably did not wish to see me let alone the baby. I always bring you grief. I do not see how you could ever keep loving me." Clara said to me as she took my handkerchief from me.

I looked at her with sad eyes and tilted her chin up so her eyes could investigate mine. "Doubt thou the stars are fire, Doubt that the sun doth move, Doubt truth to be a liar, but never doubt I love." William Shakespeare. Act II, Scene II. Never doubt my love for you Clara. Out of anything else and all the sins I make never doubt that. I will gladly go to Hell and back for you. Every beating I have ever gotten for loving you is worth it. I will never stop loving you. So, whatever the Royal Wizard Council brings, and I must face for my affair with you I will gladly take it and any other crimes they charge me with. It will all be well worth it to free you. At least for a moment."

Tears rolled down her cheeks as she searched my face to see if I was lying. After I assumed being convinced of my truth she leaned in and kissed my lips. Her lips were soft and tender as she deepened the kiss more as if it could be our last kiss and it very well could be. If Noah wasn't in the room, I would have gladly taken her right then and worked to push every worry and thought out of her mind as I made love to her, but it seemed that would have to wait.

Reluctantly I pulled away and rested my forehead on hers.

"Let us go down and eat. I am sure you have not been eating like you should be. You are looking pale and frail." I said to her.

I am sure she caught on to the concern in my voice from the look she gave me. Her hand gently cupped my cheek and I leaned into her touch that I had been missing more than I could ever admit. "I am sorry I have worried you. I have missed you. I do not plan to go back, at least not willingly. I am tired of being ripped away from you in every life." Kissing the palm of her hand as she spoke to me, I could tell she meant it. The hurt behind her words and in her eyes said it all. "But yes, we should go down… I can't remember the last time I really ate."

I frowned at her words and shook my head. "Clara, you have to eat…"

"I know. I just haven't had much of an appetite. Please do not look at me like that."

"How can I not? I worry for you… and for Noah."

She looked over at Noah who was curled up laying on top of Amethyst sucking his thumb with sleepy eyes, "they look sweet together." She had a soft smile that graced her perfect pink lips.

I was about to respond when I heard my phone ring and saw Jenna's name pop up on my screen. Clara and I exchanged a slight worried look as I answered it. Pressing the phone to my ear I let out a shaky breath and held Clara closely to me. "Jenna?"

"Daniel. Hey…"

"Can I talk to them? Is that Daniel?"

"Chester… will you stop. Sit down." I heard Jenna scold and a slight pout come from Chester on the other end. "Sit down with Heather an' chill. You're like an over excited Lab."

"You're just as cranky as Daniel."

"I resent that." I finally chimed in because it was clear I was on speaker. "Who is Heather?"

"Chester's new girlfriend he has, him an' Stevie broke up after disagreements on you." Jenna's Scottish accent was strong as she spoke to me, and Chester's was just as thick. "Anyways… they are lookin' for you an' for Clara. We wouldn' tell them where you both was but you had best be on the lookout. When they find ya they plan to bring you in Daniel. They found information on you… they plan to charge you for murder to royals you have killed that have ties with the Royal Wizard Counsel an' others that you have committed in the past."

I was silent. I pierced my lips together and I felt Clara clinch on to me tightly and start to shake. "I see…"

"Argon and the other immortals are trying to fight for you and clear your name just as Romeo is… well Arthur."

"Thank you, Jenna. It seems my time is running out on stopping Ophelia…"

"Sebastian is still working on sealing things away as well. He isn' really talking to Chester and I because we believe in you. We will come to where you are and help you. The three of us are getting our bags packed now."

"You do not have to do that. The more you associate with me the more you could be pinned for anything else they charge me with."

"I do not quite frankly care. They can kiss my Scottish arse for all I care. They are a bunch of uptight wankers."

"I second that. Y'er our mate Daniel. We aren't lettin' them get away with this. Even if you can be a right arse yourself."

I chuckled at their response. My chest was tight at hearing them defend me and caring to help. It was a kindness I wasn't too familiar with, at least not in a long time. "Thank you both." I said softly into the phone and kissed the top of Clara's head. "Safe travels." They both were the only two aside from the immortals and Romeo that knew where I was. I had not even told my mother. I thought it was safer that she did not know. Hanging up the phone I looked back at Noah and Amethyst, "let us get them and you downstairs to eat."

"Well Noah still takes a bottle. He is slowly starting to try soft foods." Clara walked over and picked Noah up into her arms only for him to hold his arms out for me to take him. A sad smile rested on my lips as I took him from her. "He seems to like you." She said softly.

"It appears so." I held him gently in my arms and he played with the amethyst that hung around my neck. His little fingers wrapped around the raw crystal and his big blue eyes stayed locked on it. Amethyst hopped off the bed and faded away in glittery light into my ring that gave a moment of soft glow letting me know he was taking a much-needed rest after being out longer than he needed to be. Even after he was set free, and I broke the connection he still left weaker if he had not been in the ring recharging. He was a spell I manifested as a small boy, a link to me and my magick. We were one.

Chapter 4

Walking into the dining room of the Bed and Breakfast, I caught sight of MaryBell nudging Jud to get his attention when we entered. I let Clara get sat first as I kept Noah in my arms. He still had one little hand held tightly on my necklace while the other hand had his thumb popped in his mouth sucking softly on it. I caught him always looking up at me and he would smile at me showing his little dimples. Little giggles would escape his mouth that he still had his thumb in when I would look back at him and give him an amused smile.

Feeling a heavy hand rest on my shoulder Jud chuckled and patted my shoulder. "The kids did always like ya Elijah... I mean Merlin. Sorry."

"It is okay. I would imagine it will take some getting used to, for everyone."

Jud gave me a nod in understanding, "so this is your girl you told me about and her littlen'. Cute kid. He favors you, Merlin."

Shaking my head, I gave a chuckle. "Hardly."

Clara let a soft blush grace her face as a sad smile lingered over her lips.

"And she is right pretty. Hard to believe she would go for an ugly mug like yours." A mischievous smile sat on Jud's face as he gave me a wink letting me know he was only teasing. "Nah, I'm jus' messin' with ya son. You both make a pretty couple. Anyways what can I start ya both off with?"

"We will both have tea. The same as I had it last night please for mine but for her she will want honey for her tea. What would you like to eat?"

Clara let her eyes linger over the menu. I could tell she wasn't in the mood to eat but knew I would make her anyway. "Could I please have two eggs over easy with avocado slices?"

"Of course, you can. Now what about you?"

"Eggs benedict and a scone please."

"Anything for littlen' here?"

"No thank you. I am about to fix him a bottle." Clara pulled out a bottle from the bag she had for him and poured formula into it. Noah poked his head up excitedly and his little legs went to kicking as he bounced up and down in my arms watching Clara closely fix his bottle.

Jud and I both laughed at Noah's excited antics.

"Alright. I will be right back with your teas then." Jud walked away from us and went into the kitchen where I saw MaryBell peeking out the little

window to see us. I could see the worry in her old eyes for us and her curiosity.

"Okay little one. Want to come to me so mummy can feed you?" Clara held out her hands to be able to take Noah, but he wouldn't go to her.

"I can feed him. I do not mind." I held my free hand out to take the bottle from her. Popping the bottle in his mouth I watched him use his own little hands to help hold up his bottle. "Clever little one, aren't you?" I said softly as I watched him study my face closely and then one of his hands wrapped around one of my fingers. I looked back at Clara who was watching us. I could tell she was holding back tears. "Please do not cry Clara." I said to her softly. "Everything will be okay."

"How? How are you so sure? You heard Jenna…"

"I just do. Now trust me. It will all be okay. Once I solve and stop what is going on here, we will move on to the next location. I want you to stay close to here and with Jenna and Heather when they get here. Leave things to Chester and me. I plan to place a ward on this place to help keep the owners safe. They are old friends of mine."

"I caught wind of that… okay… I believe you but Merlin… be careful…. It isn't just Ophelia after you now… it is the whole Royal Magick Counsel."

"I know…" I looked away from her and down at Noah who played with my fingers as he drank from his bottle. His blue eyes looked up to lock on to mine and he reached his small hand up to touch my face and seemed to keep it there.

The sound of our teacups being placed down on the table caught my attention and I looked up to see MaryBell and Jud. MaryBell had a deep look of worry on her face, and she gently rested her hand on my shoulder. "Everything will be fine ma'am." I said to her gently.

"I know you say that, but I still can't help but worry." Her hand moved to stroke the top of Noah's curly blonde hair that covered his little head. He had Wesley's hair. I could see a lot of the young king in the baby, but he still had a lot of Clara's features as well. "So young, so innocent. How are you sweetie?" She asked Clara. "You can stay here as long as you need. Both of you. We will watch over y'all."

"I am fine ma'am, thank you for your kindness." Clara replied to her as she held her teacup nervously.

"Oh, how rude of me. I am MaryBell. You already met my husband Jud. We knew Elijah a long time ago."

"MaryBell I told you his real name is Merlin."

"I know but I will always know him by our Elijah. The kids were crazy over him growing up. They always enjoyed his stories about faraway kingdoms and a brave king and his wizard and an even braver princess. I guess the stories wasn't just fairytales to get the kids to go to bed."

I licked my lips and gave a sad chuckle at her words and locked eyes with Clara who stayed looking into her teacup. I watched as tears dripped into her tea, but she didn't say anything. "No, not quite."

"You know, we are pretty good with kids. Had a house full you know. We could watch this little guy if you two need a moment." Jud said to us, and I looked up at him with a slight embarrassed look. "Just think about it." He gave me a wink and gently patted Clara's shoulder. "They have a play t'night at the old Thalian Hall in town. Why not take her out? I remember you used to read those plays. You always was reading when we was deployed and even after. Always had your nose in a book."

Clara shyly looked up at me and gave me a sheepish smile as she cleaned her tears away.

"I did not always have... oh never mind." I scowled and looked at Clara letting my scowl fall away. "What do you say Clara? Care to let me court you tonight?"

She bit her lower lip and blushed a shade darker and gave a nod, "I would very much enjoy that. Thank you... to both of you."

"Well, we kept wondering when he was going to bring a girl over to visit with him. Didn't think it would be a decade later though and like this. I was startin' to think you might of swung the other way and was too embarrassed to tell us."

"Jud!" Mary Bell scolds.

I rolled my eyes and let out a sigh. Clara's laughter at the old couple and Jud's teasing amused her. Hearing her laughter was music to my ears.

"What is so fun?" I mused.

"Oh nothing." She quips back with a smile on her face that made my heart skip a beat.

"Is that so?" I questioned and looked her over biting my lower lip and chuckling to myself.

"Back to the kitchen to check on your food. Jud get the little one from them so they can eat."MaryBell said as she hurried off.

"Alight squirt. Come to Pawpa. Nannie went to check on the food. Think we can sneak you a bit of the good stuff behind the counter?" Jud said as he took Noah in his arms causing the baby to giggle and squeal excitedly as he reached for Jud's glasses. Jud laughed himself as he acted like he was sneaking behind the counter where pastries were on display that he had been eyeballing.

Shaking my head at the two I chuckled and went about fixing my tea. Being in Jud and MaryBell's home felt like home. It was warm and welcoming. They treated me as if I were family. I had missed this feeling. The feeling of being safe, loved, and welcomed.

"Drat, they locked it on us Noah." I heard Jud say as I looked up to watch him try to open the door to the display.

"Judson Knight. What do you think you are doing?" MaryBell snips as she comes out with our breakfast. Jud held up his free hand to play innocent. "It was the baby."

"Uh-huh. Don't you blame that baby for your sweet tooth. You know you have to watch your sugar." She sat our plates down in front of us. "I swear. I don't know what I'm gonna do with him." She chuckled and smiled at us. "He's a mess."

Baby laughter could be heard throughout the dining room as Jud played with Noah.

"He has not changed." I replied and took a sip of my tea. I felt at peace in this moment. The first time in a long time I felt at complete peace watching Jud with Noah and being back with them. I was home. "Thank you MaryBell…."

She looked back at me and rested her hand on my head and ruffled my hair. "Welcome home Elijah. I know your real name, but you will always be our Elijah…." She sighs and drops her hand. "Back to work. I have some cooking to get finished and more to plan for a wedding tomorrow night that will be here."

"A wedding?" Clara questioned. "How wonderful!"

"It is. We are catering it. The decorators will be coming in to fix up the formal dining room and the courtyard out back. A lovely fall wedding."

"It will be right purdy." Jud chimes in as he comes back over to us.

MaryBell rolled her eyes at his teasing notion as he kissed the top of her head before she walked back into the kitchen. He had a big playful smile on his face as he sat down with us and bounced Noah on his knee.

"You have one beautiful baby Clara."

"Thank you, sir."

"Please, call me Jud."

"Jud."

"How often do you get to see your grandchildren Jud?" I asked as I took a bite of my breakfast.

"A decent bit. Sundays mostly. We all go to church together then come home and have Sunday lunch together. Why don't you both come to service with us Sunday? The kids will love to see you."

"Oh… I do not know Jud…"

"C'mon, we'll all go together as a family."

"Yes, but I have work to do. Ever since I got here, I have been feeling a dark energy. It is strong and it is pushing against whatever light is weakly trying to push back. I would say it must be the spirits that linger in this town that is trying to win out, but their spiritual energy is not holding up. I need to stop whatever is going on here and quickly before it spreads and consumes everything in its path."

Jud frowns at my response as he let Noah play with the rings he wore on his hand and one being a Mason ring on his pinky ring that Noah seemed to like the most.

"Merlin…." Clara reached over and took my hand.

"If I do not stop the darkness then who will?"

"I know but that does not stop me from worrying over you, but you are still not in this alone."

"As I said I will place a ward on this place… I want you to stay here. All of you. When Chester gets here tomorrow, he and I will go and investigate. All of you try not to leave the property. I know you have a wedding tomorrow. Be cautious. The ward will keep out the darkness and evil if it tries to enter."

They both sat silently and all that could be heard was the noises of Noah trying to blow bubbles that only made drool run down his chin and squeal excitedly. Jud cleaned his little chin only for Noah to take Jud's finger and try to chew on it.

"I believe you have a teether here." Jud said with a chuckle. He glanced back at me. "I will keep an eye on things here son… don't you worry. Your sweetheart is in good hands. Maybe I can talk her into helping me break into the pastry cabinet."

Clara giggled at the old man's sweet notions as she pulled out a teething toy for Noah and passed it to Jud. "I am not sure Mrs. MaryBell would appreciate that too much Jud."

"Nah. She doesn' have to know."

"Well, it seems you'll be causing trouble tomorrow while I am away." I teased in response. "That has not changed."

"Trouble? Me? Never."

"Yes you."

"Merlin, I think you are the one losing it in your old age."

I scoffed and took another bite or two. Clara covered her mouth and giggled as she listened to us banter back and forth.

"Are they giving you a hard time Clara? I could put these two to work washing the dishes and we can take our tea and coffee out on the back patio with the baby. Let him crawl around and play." MaryBell came back in from the kitchen and sat beside Clara. "My turn to hold the baby. You heard me. Get going you two. The dishes won't wash themselves and none of that hocus pocus to cheat to get it done."

"She isn' joking, is she?"

"She is your wife. You would know better than I would but no."

Jud gave a sigh and got up passing Noah to MaryBell.

"There we are come to Nannie. Now what have you been up to bunkin?"

I took mine and Clara's plate with me as I followed Jud into the kitchen. "I blame you for us getting into trouble." I said to him teasingly and dumped the food then placed the fine china into the sink.

Catching an apron, he tossed me I slipped it on. "Let's get to it before she comes in here and cracks the whip."

I rolled my eyes and chuckled. "We could sneak, and I can have this done quickly…"

"Now what did I say?"

I jumped and looked back and down at the short woman holding Noah.

"Where did you come from? How did I not hear you?"

"Looks like you're losing your touch Merlin." Clara teased from where she was leaning on the counter.

"I came to get my coffee. Now both of you better wash those dishes good." I gave Clara a look and slightly licked my lips and half laughed. She bit her lower lip and looked away with a mischievous smile on her face. "Yes ma'am."

"I'm watching you, Elijah. No funny business. The same goes for you too Judson." MaryBell wagged her finger at us. "Clara sweetpea can you grab my coffee cup?" She nods to the full cup of hot coffee on the counter. Taking the mug, they left the kitchen.

Jud and I looked at one another and started to laugh.

"I'm glad you're back."

"So am I… I have missed being around you both."

"You never had to hide from us Merlin. You're family."

"I am sorry…was not sure… it is a lot to take in and understand. A lot about me I am still not sure of even after all this time as passed."

"Either way we still love you. You're family and family takes care of one another."

We both fell silent as the clinking of dishes and running water filled the silence between us.

"How are you going to stop this darkness thing?" Jud finally asked me.

"I am going to seal whatever it is away, find where its power source is coming from and shut it down."

"There has also been a string of missing persons in town." He said to me in a low voice. "All young women. Around your girl's age. Teenage to early and mid-twenties. The tourist level has been dropping. Not just because of that virus but because of them girls going missin'. Now I don't know if that has anythin' to do with what you got yourself involved in, but I do know it is getting worse."

I took in his words and gave a curt nod, "I am sure it has to do with what is going on. Last year the girls were being used as a sacrifice in a ritual performed by Ophelia. She might be doing it again. To complete it to bring back Lord Thomas and free Areses... Only one of those she might win at bringing back."

Silence sat back in again.

Drying my hands off I looked at the old clock hanging on the wall. Lunch would soon have to be started.

"C'mon, let's go see the girls. The lunch staff can handle things from here." Jud took his apron off and held the kitchen door open for me to follow. Pulling the apron off and folding up neatly I rested it on the counter then followed him out.

Finding our way out onto the back patio we found MaryBell and Clara chatting as Noah played on his blanket that was spread out. He had two leaves in his hands that he was waving around and making excited sounds.

"I see you both finally finished." MaryBell quips.

"Of course, why would we not?" Jud leant down and kissed the top of her head before taking a set next to her.

Noah started to bounce up and down as he reached his arms up for me to take him with big eyes that seemed almost pleading. I leaned down and scooped him up and gently tossed him in the air as he giggled and yelled out excitedly. Holding him close to me I smiled down at him and laughed at his sweet notions. Catching Clara's expression, I watched her slightly blush as she watched me with Noah.

"He's always been good with kids." MaryBell leans in saying to her. "You three make a pretty family."

Clara bit her lower lip, and her blush got a little more red. "Why are you blushing?"

"I'm not." Clara replied quickly to me.

"Yes, you are."

"No, I am not."

"We can work on making another one of these later if you fancy." I gave her a smirk and a wink. I watched her mouth drop open and her face turn bright red. I chuckled at her expression.

"Merlin!"

Jud chuckled and MaryBell gave him a slight smack on his arm. "Now don't encourage him."

"What did I say?" I teased.

Clara sighed heavily and shook her head hiding her face behind her hands. Taking Noah, I walked over to her and gently lowered her hands from her face and tilted her chin up so I could investigate her celestial orbs. I leaned in and kissed her lips tenderly. Slowly pulling away I rested my forehead on hers.

"I love you." I whispered to her and took the set next to her.

"And I love you."

Jud and MaryBell exchanged a sad look between them before looking back at us.

"But you are right. He is wonderful with children. Always has been. Even back in Camelot. One little boy and girl took a very big liking to him. Do you remember that?"

"Sergio and Scarlet. Sergio was the oldest. Scarlet was the youngest. They were also magically gifted. Sergio worked at the palace as a stable boy if my memory serves me right."

"Yes. He looked up to you. It was adorable. All the village kids would play together. All the boys wanted to be knights but not Sergio. He wanted to be you."

I chuckled and rubbed the back of my neck as I remembered the young lad and his sister. "That he did."

"Sounds like you had a little fan base." MaryBell teased.

"I guess you can say that."

"And this little one right here is definitely taken with you." She went on. I looked down at Noah who was now sleeping in my arms sucking his thumb. Soft snores left him as I watched him sleep. The autumn breeze danced around us rustling the leaves. "And I am taken with him." I waved my hand to have his blanket brought to me and I covered him up to keep the chill from the air off him.

"Mrs. Knight!" The girl from last night ran up to where we were in the garden. Slight jealousy washed over her at the sight of Clara and I with Noah.

"What is it, Tiffany?" MaryBell asked as she got to her feet.

She ripped her eyes from us and looked back at MaryBell, "The orchestra canceled for tomorrow for the wedding."

"What! Why?"

"Something about being too worried about being in this town with the spike in crime."

"What will we do the wedding is tomorrow?"

"It's okay we will figure something out."

"How? This is last minute, and we are not prepared with a backup."MaryBell replied to Jud.

"Just breathe." Jud looks at me. "I know you can play piano and you showed me Clara playing the violin. Can you both stand in?"

I looked at him shocked.

"And you sing. Both of you can."

Still, I was shocked. Was I really about to agree to do this? This is not what I had in mind to do tomorrow but the look of desperation on MaryBell's face made me cave.

"Please Merlin... you know I would not ask this of you both if we didn't really need the help."

I hesitated.

"We would be happy to help." Clara spoke for us both. "Also means I get to stop you from going off and getting into trouble." She said to me.

I rolled my eyes and let out a heavy sigh. "Okay. Fine. It seems I have no say so in the matter. We will help. But let us not make this something that happens all the time."

"Oh, don't be so grumpy, you have plenty of time to go save the world."

I gave Clara a side glance and a slight smirk. She only responded with sticking her tongue out at me.

The two elderly couple chuckled at us. I looked back at them and gave a slight chuckle myself.

"Now then, why don't you both get ready for your date. We will watch little man here. He will be good and spoiled by nannie and pawpa by the time you both get back." MaryBell said to us and gently took Noah from my arms. "Tiffany let everyone know the new arrangements please. I will contact the bride to let her know what is going on."

Tiffany gave me a jealous look over before ripping her eyes away to give MaryBell a fake smile and nod before turning on her heels to go make the arrangements. I rubbed my chin and furrowed my brow. I knew something was off with her and something was blocking me from reading her thoughts to know just what it was.

"Elijah…. Merlin, sorry. That will take some getting used to." Jud got to his feet and clapped his hand on my shoulder. "Come with me. I have something to show you." He had a mischievous look in his old gray eyes. "Don't worry I'll getcha back to your girl in time for this date of yours." I got up and gave a slight chuckle. Leaning down I gave Clara a kiss on her cheek and then kissed the top of Noah's head. "Seems I will see you a little later. Stay out of trouble." I said to her teasingly.

She gave a scoff, "me? Have you met you?" Her laughter was music to my ears and her smile was unforgettable. "You stay out of trouble mister." She got to her feet and leaned up to kiss me gently on my lips. The soft brush sent chills down my spine and made my body ache.

"Ahmm." The sound of someone clearing their throat pulled me out of the small moment. Looking over I saw Jud watching us and waiting for me to follow him. MaryBell's soft laugh could be heard behind me. I couldn't help but let out a slight chuckle of my own.

"Right. Of course." I looked back down at Clara. "I will see you both in a bit." I kissed her cheek one more time and followed alongside Jud who was walking up a path through the garden to a barn. "What do you need to show me Judson?"

"I saw that you came in on that motorcycle of yours. You can't take yer girl out on that. Need something proper."

Taking out his keys he unlocked the large stall doors and I helped him pull it back. The fall afternoon sunlight broke the darkness in the barn casting light over something that was covered up. I arched my brow and looked over at him.

Flipping a switch, the lights came on in the barn he walked over and pulled back the tarp that had covered what was under it. I couldn't help but let out a surprised laugh and let a smile move over my face.

"Now then. This 67 Chevy is overdue for a night out on the town. What do you say?" Jud tossed me the keys to the sleek black car with a leather top and leather interior to match.

I looked at the keys in my hands and back at Jud. "Are you serious?"

"As a heart attack."

I looked over the classic car that was in perfect condition and licked my lips in slight excitement that I was embarrassingly enough trying to contain. "What are you waiting for? Get in and start her up!"

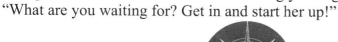

Looking back at the old man I saw the amusement on his face at my expression. I moved quickly into the driver's seat and slid the keys into the ignition switching the car on. Hearing the engine come to life made both him and I smile and laugh. It all felt normal. For once in a long, long-time things felt normal. I felt normal. My chest felt tight as I ran my hands over the black steering wheel taking in every precious moment from the time I got to Wilmington. In just a few short hours of being in town and finding my old friends I felt at peace again. I felt like I was normal, wanted, like I belonged somewhere. Only thing was, I knew it was not going to last. Nothing good in my life ever seemed to last. It is always ripped away from me. Time and time again.

"Are you okay Merlin?" Jud was in the passenger seat next to me. When he slid in next to me, I'm not sure but I looked over at him and saw he had a worried look. "You're crying."

I touched my face in surprise and realized I was. Rubbing my eyes and cleaning away the tears quickly I let out an embarrassed laugh. "My apologies."

"Why? You have nothin' to be sorry for son."

I looked away from him and ran my fingers through my hair.

"You've had a hard life haven' you?"

"You can say that."

"Well…. You always will have a home here. No judgment. No questions. This is your home also. You have always had a place here old friend."

I gave a sad but grateful nod. "Thank you."

"I am also going out on a limb here and assume you haven't had a normal moment in a long time."

"You would be right."

"I see."

"Really Judson… thank you."

"You don't have to thank me. I'm just glad to have gotten to see you again before I passed away."

"You are not going anywhere old man." I looked back at him with a half-smile.

With a chuckle and shake of his head. "Son… as much as I have enjoyed life when it is my time to go, I am ready. I will go and wait under that cryin' tree in the sky for my sweetheart to join me. I know she will be here a while."

Something about his words stung. The thought of him not being here anymore made my chest ache as I listened to him. "Well, I hope it isn't for a very long time Judson."

"Me too."

"Are you sure you are okay with me driving your car? She is truly a beauty. A classic."

"Of course, I am. You're going to need a car for your little family."

"Excuse me?" I looked at him confused at his choice of words.

Jud chuckled at my expression. "I'm giving you this here Chevy."

I looked at him shocked. It wasn't like I could not afford to get one myself. Aside from that they can be hard to come by in perfect condition like his has been kept in, but I have not needed a car. I have been on my own for a while. "Judson... at least let me buy it from you."

"Keep yer money, Merlin. I don' need it. You just promise to come around more often and bring that baby with you. Maybe give us another one hmm?" The last part he said teasingly.

I did not know how to respond. I pulled my thoughts together and gave him a sad smile, "she is married to another Judson. I- as much as... I love her Judson. I cannot ever see myself in any life with another. My soul knows her soul and her mine... she is my soulmate, but we continue in each life she is born into.... we keep being ripped apart from one another and I continue to let her down and not be the man that she deserves."

Jud sat next to me and was silent for a moment. He let out a heavy sigh and ran a hand over his face, "Merlin I can't pretend to know everything you have been through, but I do know one thing and that is that Clara is crazy about you. In those lives you chose to show me she holds the same look she always has for you. To her you are and always will be her soulmate. We all do wrong, but it is how we can change it and do it right, so we don't make those same mistakes again. You can't save everyone Merlin. You just need to save one... and a half."

I looked over at him quickly and furrowed my brows taking in what he was saying.

"Now you need to go get ready for this date of yours." Jud went on and clapped his hand over my shoulder.

"Yes... I suppose so." I swallowed hard and licked my lips, "thank you Judson."

Chapter 5

I was nervous. For the first time in a long time did things feel normal but I knew it wouldn't last long, nothing good ever did. I sat on an old purple Victorian sofa playing with my ring waiting for Clara to come down. Hearing footsteps coming down the stairs I looked up to see Clara. I couldn't take my eyes off her, she was enchanting to me. The dark midnight blue vintage style tee length dress captured her eyes and made them shine. A soft tint of pink graced her cheeks when she noticed my eyes looking her over.

"Is it too much?" She asked me and averted her eyes.

"N-no... I'm sorry. I- you're just so beautiful. You always seem to leave me breathless." I managed to say to her as I got to my feet to make my way over to her.

She bit her lower lip and played with her fingers nervously as she listened to my words. "Thank you." She whispered out.
Holding my hand out for her to take it she placed her soft hand in mine. "You are always so beautiful to me. No matter how many lives you have and times your appearance changes... are you ready to go my love?"

Clara gave a shy nod in response and wrapped her arms around mine to hug it. Smiling down at her I kiss the top of her head.
"Have fun and be safe you two." I looked. Over my shoulder to see the elderly couple with Noah in Jud's arms and a mischievous smile on the old man's face, "and don't you two worry. We can handle little man here."

"Thank you both." I reply and let out a chuckle at Noah trying to still get a hold of Jud's glasses, "we best be off, or we will be late to the show."
Letting go of my arm Clara went and gave Noah a kiss on top of his curly blonde head before joining me at the door again. Holding the door open for her to go out first I looked back at Jud one more time. He gave me a reassuring smile and nodded for me to go on. Why I was nervous, I didn't know. It wasn't like I was not used to being with her. Taking her hand in mine I nodded for her to follow me to the Impala. I held her car door open for her and let her slide in on the passenger side before I got in.

Getting in on the driver side I cranked the car. The sound of the classic car still gave me chills to hear and a small smile creep over my lips at it and being behind the wheel.

"Do I need to give you two a moment?" Clara's voice sang out and broke my train of thought.
Looking over at her she had an amused look on her face that I responded to with an embarrassed smile and chuckle, "sorry. No... I- uh... shit." I shook my head and backed pulled out getting on the main road.

Clara giggled at my response, "What? Merlin is embarrassed that I caught him having a moment. Who would have thought?"
"I was not..."
"It is okay. I get it. You have another love interest in your life aside from that motorbike of yours."
"Okay leave her out of this."
"What? It is beautiful. What year was it again? 1956?"
I gave a sigh, "yes."
"I am okay with you cheating on me with your little toys."
"Cheating?" I looked at her in shock only for her to burst out laughing at me. "You are being a brat. You know that?"
"Mhmm, what are you going to do about it?" I could hear the teasing challenge in her voice.

I licked my lips and let out a chuckle as I watched the road. "Do not worry. I will be more than happy to deal with you when we get back to my room. Until then I need you to be able to walk for right now." Side glancing at Clara I watched her shift slightly in her seat causing a smirk to form on my lips, "did I strike a nerve Princess?" I looked over at her as I reached my hand over and let it start to slightly move the end of her skirt up and into her inner thigh just barely missing her delicate area. My skin brushing against hers, the sound of her taking in a sharp breath at my touch. Pulling my hand away I pull into a parking spot parking the car. I looked over at her seeing her flustered and working to compose herself. I leaned forward to whisper into her ear. "Are you going to behave yourself or do I need to handle you a bit more harshly than just a tease of touching?"

A slight whimper left her lips as she chewed on her lower lip, "no... no.... um." She shifted more in her seat as my fingers lingered at the end of her skirt, "we... we should get out."

"Are you going to behave?" I asked her again moving my fingers up her inner thigh to her panties and pressed my index finger to where her clit was and watched her face carefully as it flushed over, and a moan escaped her lips. She was already getting wet, and it was hard to not want to take her and have my way with her right then, but I reframed from doing it.

"Y-yes-s yes sir." She quickly covered her mouth at her choice of word. I pulled my hand away and chuckled at her adorable notions. Slipping out the driver side to go around and open her door I hold my hand out for her to take and get out.

We walked the sidewalk to with her taking my arm to hug. I toyed with the topic I had in mind that I wanted to ask her. It was even in a memory that had recently come back to me that I had forgotten.

Hesitating I finally asked, "Clara, can I ask you something?"

She looked up at me and I could tell she was studying my face with her own eyes that filled with worry. "Of course."
"How much of your past lives do you remember?"
I stopped and pulled her off to the side as I watched her. I could tell she had started to remember a lot. She had just not shared it.
"Almost all of them..." She whispered, "down to my true name and who I was when this soul was first made. Pravuil... or also known as Vretil. The Archivist to God himself..." Clara said dryly, "Until he made me decide between you or keeping my status as a divine person. I think he blamed me for who I was meant to be with becoming one of the Fallen Seven." She licked her lips and let out a shaky breath as her eyes darted around the street and then back to me. "I remember being Sophia... and what happened to me... what they did to you..." Her voice started to tremble, and I quickly pulled her in to hold her.

"Shhhshhh, calm down. I am sorry I brought it up... I should have waited. Are you hungry? We have a little time before the show." I asked her gently feeling her start to calm down in my arms. She gave a nod in response to my question and pulled away slightly only to take my arm to hug to her again and nuzzle into. Smiling down at her I kissed the top of her head and lead the way to a restaurant that Jud had recommended.

I held the door open to Circa1922 that I had made reservations for. I know I had asked her if she was hungry. I only made the reservations to be on the safe side. Giving the hostess my name and watching her look me over a bit too much we finally got sat at our table. Pulling Clara's chair out I let her sit first before taking mine across from her the hostess sat our menus on the table and named off their specials. Giving her a nod, she went on her way I reached across the table to take Clara's hand in mine to play with her finger. She looked at my ring and ran her thumb over it.

"You have never been without this… well, that isn't true. You had it during your first life." She looked back at me with gentle loving eyes, "I love you, Merlin."

"And I love you Princess."

For the next hour we ate and chatted. Her laughter was always music to my ears. Every smile and touch from her made my heart skip a beat. I could never get enough of it.

Taking her hand after paying I helped her up to head out of the beautiful restaurant.
"Thank you." Clara said to me.
"What are you thanking me for?" I asked in a chuckle.
"I… I don't know?" She blushed and it only made me laugh a little more, "Now Merlin Pintikelly you best stop teasing me." She scolded me.
"Okay, okay. My apologies." I bit my lower lip as I watched a cute scowl cross her features. Walking up the steps of the theater I held the door open for her to go in first. The building was large and grand with old architecture. It had several different rooms, but we were going to the main theater to sit up on the balcony level. The deep red curtains draped around in archways and across the stage. The pillars and crown molding gave way to the age of the of the building that had been established in the 1800's. A large chandelier hung in the center of the theater lit up brightly till it was time for the show to start. We took our seats in the corner left balcony closest to the stage to watch the play that would soon start.

From the corner of my eye, I caught sight of red hair vanishing behind the curtain that was behind us. Rubbing my eyes, I look back to see it was gone. "Merlin? Is everything okay?" She questioned with worry in her voice.

"Yes, of course. Eyes are just bothering me is all." I lied and looked back at the stage where I see the figure in full this time. My heart dropped as those green eyes locked onto my blue ones. She held the same mischievous look before she vanished from sight. I gave Clara a side glance, but I could tell she didn't see anything. I was starting to think I was imagining it. Imagining her. The guilt of her death ate at me every day.

The light dimmed and the stage was set as the play started. I worked to focus my mind back on the play. On Romeo and Julliet. Only, I couldn't. No matter how hard I tried. The sight of that girl ate away at me. It haunted me.

"Merlin... are you sure you're, okay? You look as if you have seen a ghost." Clara leans over and whispers to me.

"Yes, no need to fret my dear Clara."

Even in the dim light I could see a small frown grace her lips. I knew she didn't believe me, but she didn't question it. At least not yet.

"Merlin."

I hear a loud whisper call out to me and I recognized the voice. *'"Estella." I said in my mind picking up on where she was at hovering next to me.*

"So, you did see me."

"What are you doing here? You should have passed on."

"Why should I? You need my help, and my ex is being a dick and not talking to you soooo, here I am and awe you two are so cute. Tell Clara I said hi!"

"Estella, I am not... I will later. Why do you want to help me?" I rubbed my chin as I watched the play go on with Romeo sneaking to see Juliet.

I heard Stella give a sigh next to me, "because. You need more in your corner. I know everything that is going on and I also came to tell you the counsel knows where you are at, and they are coming. They got hold of something... oh what was the name... Sompero... they're going to use it on you. It would put you in an eternal slumber. Merlin, you must leave this town tonight. You can't stay!"

I took in a sharp breath. I thought I had hidden that object away, but it seemed I was wrong. Unless Sebastian had managed to make one himself from the books of mine, he had gained from me when we were on good terms. I take Clara's hand in mine and gave it a gentle squeeze. *"I see, let them come. I am tired of running. I am trying to save this goddamn planet... this is where it ends."*

Estella walked in front of me with big worried green eyes. "Merlin if they get their hands on you... they won't care who is around... they want you basically dead. Mostly Wesley."

"Yes, I am well aware of that."

"Merlin... just think about it. I know you have the immortals in your corner helping you... and Jenna... Romeo, well Arthur.... and others... and um... um... please Merlin... we can't lose you.... Not again. Clara can't take it if you go missing a second time." She rambled out to me. I could see she was close to tears, and it made my chest tighten at her expression and her words.

"Estella..."

"It's Stella." She corrected me.

"Stella. I am sorry but I must stay. You know as well as I do something dark is here in this town. I know you can feel it. If all the other spirits here can and it is pulling and even deleting them from even being ghost, then it is something far worse than that pathetic counsel can even comprehend because it is ran by idiots that have a vendetta against me."

Clara gently squeezed my hand back and rested her head on my shoulder, "I know something is wrong Merlin. Please tell me what it is after the show." She whispered to me in a sad voice.

"Of course, my love." I kissed the top of her head. Looking back at Estella I could see the worry and sadness in her eyes.

We said no more on the topic as we watched the play till the very end. The curtain closed and the light came back up. Clara and I both got to our feet but we both stayed silent till we got out of the crowed of people and out of the building onto the sidewalk.

"Okay, tell me." Clara demanded.

I looked around and back at her taking her hand leading her back to the Impala. "Not here. Let's get in the car and I will tell you."

"Um... okay."

Pulling out the car keys I got the doors unlocked and got her in first before I got in on the driver's side. It all felt rushed, and I honestly did not want to tell her what I had learned. I started to back out and saw Estella in the backseat with those same worried green eyes watching us.

"Okay tell me. Now." Clara turned in her seat to face me.

"Stella is in the car with us. She is a ghost."

"Wait what?"

"Hold on, I am not done. She found out something important that you need to hear.... The Counsel has Sompero and they are planning to use it on me. They know where I am at, and they are coming here... for me."

I glanced over at Clara and saw she had paled at my words and silent tears stared to roll down her face. "Wh-what?"

"I am not going to let it happen. I promise." I said to her and reached over to take her hand in mine to bring it to my lips and kiss her fingers gently.

"I lost you before, I cannot bare to lose you again." Her voice crack and she let out a sob.

"Clara… Clara, I will not let them…" Seeing her this way broke my heart. I said no more on it all as we drove back to the bed in breakfast. Parking the car, I looked over at her and leaned over to her and tiled her chin up to investigate her tearstained face that I gently cleared away with my thumbs. Gently pulling her to me I captured her lips with mine and I kissed her deeply.

I kept hold of her as I turned off the car and pulled the keys out of the ignition before vanishing with her into my room in the inn. She looked around to find us in my room and then back up at me. I lifted her up into my arms to lay her on my bed, I looked down into her celestial blues then looked down at her pink supple lips. Leaning down I kissed her deeply. The feel of her hands pushing away my blazer that I helped pull off the rest of the way as she worked on my tie then my button down. I pulled away slightly to catch my breath to see her face slightly flushed as she looked up at me. The feel of her hands on my skin made me close my eyes at her touch. I felt her sit up and start to plant light kisses along my collarbone and then my chest causing my breathing to become ragged.

"Clara…"

"Shh… let me do this." She whispered to me.

I opened my eyes to see her pushing back her tears as she worked to remove her dress from where she had gotten up off the bed.

"Here let me help… you're trembling." I moved behind her and helped with the zipper then let the dress fall to the floor gently before pulling her back to bed with me. "What is it you want to do?" I asked in a whisper as she straddled me and started to tug at my belt, "are you sure?"

She nods and swallows back her tears, "I want to experience every moment with you. I don't want anything to end."

I take her hands in mind and pulled her down to me. Kissing her lips tenderly and cleaned her tears away that were escaping her. "Listen to me. I promise. You are never going to lose me again. No matter what I will always come back to you. In every life. Nothing will ever truly keep me from you."

Wrapping her arms around my neck she cried. I could see all her past lives with us together. Each one something has pulled us apart. I watched her memory flood with them as she cried into my chest. Running my fingers through her blonde locks I let her let it all out until she couldn't anymore. "Merlin promise, promise you will always come back to me. Don't let them or this war take you from me." Clara's voice was shaky as she spoke to me. "I promise princess, I will always come back to you." I tilted her chin up and whispered on her lips before I kissed her deeply and tenderly. I gently rolled her onto her back and trailed one of my hands down her body to her thigh as she worked to undo my belt and then worked to remove my slacks. Within moments we had finished undressing each other and were tangled under the sheets. Her fingers tangled in my hair as we kissed one another, her tongue intertwined with mine. She bit at my lower lip making a low groan slip out of my mouth. Moving to kiss down her neck I made sure to take my time as I lingered over her chest taking in each tender nipple in turn with my free hand, I let my fingers tease her nipple that I wasn't occupying with my mouth. I felt her arch her back into me as her fingers stayed tangled in my hair. Her moans fueling my lust for her. Moving down her stomach I left a trail of kisses stopping just above her tender area.

Locking my eyes on hers that looked pleading I slid two fingers into her. She quickly moved her hands over her mouth to cover up the loud moan that threatened to give us away. A chuckle left my lips at her reaction as I moved my fingers in her helping loosen her up to fit me but mostly to help her reach her first climax. I wanted her to feel every lustrous sensation I could give her and rid her mind of worry on what could come at mornings light. She squirmed under me and pushed her hips into my fingers that were soaking inside her. I felt her walls tighten around them and she started to pant.

"Let it all out." I whispered to her as she let herself let go and reach her first climax.

Removing my fingers from her I sucked them clean and slid myself into her slowly giving her time to adjust to my member in her as I slowly moved in and out of her. Clara wrapped her legs around my waist and pulled me deeper into her. Her cheeks were flushed over as she chewed on her lower lip. I cupped her cheek and kissed her tenderly as I thrusted in and out of her, moving to pull her closer to me to feel her skin on mine. I pinned her wrists above her head with one hand as my other tangled in her hair, not letting my lips leave hers. Our moans muffled by the exchange of kisses until I broke it to reposition us to move her into my lap to thrust up into her.

Her expression at the sudden change made me smirk. Once again, she tried to cover up her loud moans by muffling them with her hands over her mouth. Pulling her hands away I held them behind her back as I thrusted up into her watching her work to hold in wanting to cry out. Her walls tightened and throbbed around my member, I could feel her ready to climax again and it only made me want to keep going. I let her hands go only to feel her nails trail along my back and my chest leaving hot red streaks sending shivers along my spine. Her moans filled the room and mine mixing with them. The bed squeaked with each thrust of movement into her.

"I love you." She whispered to me before kissing me deeply and wrapping her arms around my neck.

I kissed her deeply the taste of her tongue on mine as I laid her on her back to thrust a few more times into her before the feeling was too much and I finished in her. She gripped me tightly at the sensation of me filling her insides up. Slowly pulling away from the kiss I panted slightly and looked down at her flushed face that she moved to hide in my chest. I laughed softly at her embarrassed expression.

"Tiamo mis Principessa." I kissed the top of her head and slowly moved off her to pull her into my arms to hold her.

"Promise you will still be here in the morning."

"I promise my dear. I will be here. Now get some sleep." I whispered in return. I could feel soft tears falling onto my chest. "Don't cry... I promise nothing will happen. I won't let it." She gave a nod in return.

Slowly sleep consumed us, the day's events catching up to us to pull us both under.

Chapter 6

Careful to get up and not wake Clara I slid off the bed and slipped back into my slacks from last night before taking a set at the desk in the room I was staying in. Pulling out my journal and flipping it open to a clean page I started to write.

'Time is running out and darkness is spreading across the land. Ophelia is still at large, and she will stop at nothing until she has brought the human race to its knees, with her ruling over it. Her thirst for power and vengeance has stripped away what little humanity she used to have…. sadly, I know I am the cause of it. Not only are we faced against her, but against so much more. They're all returning. They're awakening and remembering who they are… If I do not stop them who will? If they remember… if they find…' I rest my head in my hands and let out a shaky breath before looking back at Clara sleeping next to the spot, I should be rested in. Tapping my pen on my journal I look back down at the words written. The writing rushed and panicked. Matching my own feelings, *'I cannot let them take her again. I must stop them this time. At any cost.'* I scribbled down. My vision darkened over with flashbacks of one of the nights I lost her. Those seven cloaked men, the only thing showing through was their rings with the Freemason symbol on them. Her red hair hid her face as she landed in the snow with her blood blossoming like a flower into the markings on the ground from where they sacrificed her. *'Her name was Sophia then. A name and life that they deleted from history, and it was all my fault. I couldn't get to her. I couldn't save her. Her or my child she was pregnant with.'* Hearing shifting behind me I closed my journal and looked back to see Clara slowly waking up. "Good morning my dear."

"Merlin…" She said to me with beautiful sleepy blue eyes and a sweet smile that rested on her pink supple lips. The autumn sun shone through the curtains in our room at the B&B brightly making her golden locks shine. The white sheets left little to the imagination that clung to her bare skin. I got up from where I was sat at the desk and went to her on the bed. "I told you I would be here come morning." Leaning down I kissed her lips gently.

"We should get up and get down to breakfast so we can get Noah from them. Although I love this view of you."

She lifted her hand to cup my cheek and smile up at me, "you are right... I don't know about that. If you could see what I see... my view is just as beautiful."

I looked away from her slightly embarrassed as I rubbed the back of my neck. "Come. Time to get up." I got up from where I had been sat next to her and picked up my white button down from off the bed where it had been all night. "Jenna and Chester should be here."

"Oh, that's right!" She was up and slipping on a change of clothes from her bag that MaryBell must have had brought up and put in here like she knew Clara would be staying the night with me. She was right. She slipped on a navy-blue dress with dark yellow tights and a jumper to match. Slipping on her oxfords to match she looked herself over before slipping past me to brush her hair. "What?" She questioned me when she caught me watching her while I brushed my teeth.

Spitting out the toothpaste and cleaning the mess away I shook my head in amusement, "nothing. You are just beautiful to me."

"Oh..."

I chuckled and finished getting cleaned up when a knock came to the door. "Oi, Daniel." Sounded Chester from the other side of the door, "stop snogging and let us in."

"Oh Neptune. He is ridiculous."

Clara was laughing from the bathroom when I opened the door to scowl at the three on the other side.

"Oh, good yer' up. I was thinking you were still busy... ouch! What was that for Jenna?"

"Stop it, Chester. What they do alone in none of yer' business and you know it. Plus, we need to get to work, the counsel is moving quickly. They know yer' in this town Daniel but they haven' tracked you to here yet. I may have led them away for a bit. Sent them on a ghost hunt of the town."

They moved past me into the room with Heather giving me a slight shy wave.

Clara came out of the bathroom and pulled Jenna and Heather in for a hug. "I am so glad to see you three. How much time do we have? The couple that owns this place has a wedding today. We cannot let things go wrong. They're counting us to help them."

"That you volunteered us for." I pointed out. "I think I would rather take my chances with Ophelia than working a wedding."

"Oh, stop it. At least with the wards up they should not be able to get in and you are given more time to come up with a better plan than chance."

"Clara, I will be fine."

"Fine? You call what is going on fine? They are trying to do away with you in the most permanent way they can come up with. It isn't fine!"

"Clara!" I raised my voice and watched her flinch and stumble back only for Jenna to catch her. I took a deep breath and closed my eyes running my fingers through my hair. "I am sorry… I should have not raised my voice…. Look, I will be careful, okay? I cannot hide behind wards though. I know all of you can feel the shift and how bad things are and it is gathering in this town. I must stop it and those seven councilmen are not going to stand in my way. 'Seven… could they be…?'

"Daniel."

A voice broke my train of thought.

"I know you want to stop all that is going on, but we really do need to handle the counsel. They're only going to get in the way." Heather finally spoke up from where she stood with Chester. She was about the same height and build as Stevie, but she had a softer-spoken voice. She was pale and had short hair that reminded me of a pixie and hazel eyes that seemed to turn blue.

"Also, can we take this conversation downstairs? I'm starving and I can smell the food." Chester chimes in as he rubbed his stomach.

I rolled my eyes and set out a heavy sigh. "Yes, of course. We need to get Noah from Judson and MaryBell anyways." I glanced over to Clara who gave me sad eyes as she hugged onto Jenna's arm. "I am sorry Clara… I shouldn't have…" I shake my head, "never mind. Let's head down." I said gently.

Jenna gave me a stern look that I ignored as I followed them all out of the room and locked it behind me.

Walking into the dining-room I could see out the large windows that preparations for the wedding that evening was in full swing. I let out a heavy sigh at the event and what Clara had agreed for us to do.

"Good mornin' kids. I see your friends here found their way to ya." Jud came out of the kitchen with Noah in his arms.

An excited sound came out of the small child at the sight of Clara. His arms outstretched as he bounced in Jud's arms ready for his mother to take him. Clara let out a soft laugh and took Noah from Jud.

"Well, I missed you too my little mage." Clara said to him and kissed him playfully making him laugh more. He stopped when he spotted me and started to reach desperately for me.

"Daddy…"

I froze and my heart stopped. Everyone froze. He repeated that same word again and this time started to cry until I took him.

"He…"

I held Noah to me as he played with my necklace, "I- I know…" I replied to Chester who had a confused look on his face.

"Can you read his thoughts?" Jenna questioned.

"Yes…"

"To see what he is thinking."

I looked down at Noah and his blue eyes looked back up at me. He smiled a big, sweet smile and touched my face and repeated those words that made my heart tighten up. Scanning his thoughts, I took in a sharp breath.

"It- it can't be" I muttered out.

"What is it, Merlin?" Clara asked and rested her hand on my shoulder gently.

"He… he is…" I swallowed hard at what Noah had remembered and shown me, "I don't know how he remembers…"

"Merlin, breathe." Jud instructed. "Calm down and tell us what you saw."

I gave a nod and searched the smiling baby's face, "he is the reincarnation of Morgana and I's baby…. He… He remembers me trying to save him. He remembers what happened." I could hear my voice crack and my chest felt like my heart would rip apart.

"Oh, my saints…." Jenna whispered and ran her fingers through her short dark hair.

Clara covered her mouth and tears rolled down her face, "Wh-what…?"

I looked down at her blinking back tears of my own. "It is him." I whispered.

"All of you, take a seat. I will get you all something to drink." Jud said to us.

"Make mine a double." I said in a shaky voice.

"Make that two." Chester said with shock written all over his face.

Taking a seat at one of the larger tables we all sat in silent shock while Jud worked on getting us drinks. We were all in disbelief.

"How is it possible?" Heather finally asked.

"I- I don't know…" I managed to voice. I couldn't pull my eyes from Noah. Looking down at him meeting his blue eyes it was like he was trying to calm me himself as he touched my face.

"Here you all are, took the liberty in making this for the girls. Those mimosa things that the bridal party is having right now while they're up getting ready in the barn for weddings." Jud sat our drinks down for us and looked us all over with worry. "I'm not sure how to give advice on this but I look at it as a blessin' what you once lost now found its way back to ya."

"Trust me… God has not been on my side in a long, long time… not after…" I let out a heavy sigh.

Jud frowned at my words and rested a hand on my shoulder. "Anyways, what would you kids like to eat?"

We all ordered but I honestly wasn't hungry at that point. Not after finding out what I did. It felt like God was mocking me. Constantly putting one thing after another in the way of her and I being together, and I know it was because she gave up her divinity to be with me. Left who she was meant to have been with, that she never wanted to be in the first place, for me. She defied him and God for me and because of it she has had to suffer in every life.

"Daniel."

A voice called to me, and a flash of red hair broke me out of my thoughts.

"Daniel, pull yourself together. They're coming." Stella said to me, "they're close. They figured out where you are at. You have to…"

'I am not running Stella. I will deal with them when they get here but I am not running. I am tracking Ophelia and I have other problems starting to surface. I am not running.'

"Daniel, how can you face them alone? You know they would not hesitate to hurt any of these people to get to you. Jud and MaryBell don't have magick. They will kill them."

I rubbed my eyes. I knew Stella was right, but it didn't stop the fact I was not planning on running.

'They would have to get past my wards first and they won't be able to do that…'

"Daniel, they have Romeo. They plan to use him to force your hand. He is in bad shape. He isn't talking though."

54

"What?" I said out loud with shock in my voice. I quickly realized I wasn't talking in my mind anymore and all their eyes were back on me.

"Daniel?" Jenna questioned with worry.

"Stella is here, isn't she? You were talking to her again." Clara cuts in.

"Stella? Stella is a ghost?" Chester looked around trying to spot and that seemed to make Stella laugh when he went to look under the table.

"Teddy Bear she isn't under the table." Heather tapped his shoulder to have him sit up, "she is right over there." She pointed right at Stella.

Stella and I looked at each other in slight surprise.

"You can see me?"

"Yes." Heather tilted her head as she looked the redheaded girl over. "You are pretty."

"Oh, well thank you so are you."

"Okay, okay. This is cute and all but what did she say?"

"The seven councilmen have Romeo and they have hurt him. They plan to use him as ransom to make Daniel do what they want." Heather looked me over with knowing wide eyes. Her English accent was soft as she spoke to us, yet it sent chills down my spine, "you know who those men are. You have had run-ins with them in the past. Each time they take from you. Use others against you. They wear the rings of the Freemasons. Once called the Fallen Seven, then became the Seven Sages."

I swallowed hard at her words. "How did…"

"Heather can see things. She has the gift of sight." Chester explained with a mouth full of food.

"Oh, you have something on your mouth." Heather removed her eyes from mine and started to clean Chester's mouth with a napkin. "Much better, they are close Daniel. Closer than you want them to be."

I took in a sharp breath at her words.

"They're here." Stella's voice rang out in my ears.

"Damnit." My heart was pounding in my chest. I passed Noah back to Clara who looked up at me with fear written all over her face. "Stay here." I kissed her lips tenderly and pulled away.

Chester was on his feet following me with Jenna on his heels. I hadn't noticed that Jud had slipped away until I heard him coming down the stairs with a rifle.

"Judson. You cannot… is that a Smith & Wesson semiautomatic?"

"Yes sir it is, it's a-"

"Hold on. Wait, no. They will kill you. I know you have a sharp shot, but they have magick on their side."

"I know and I have you. They have to get through that ward of yours, don't they? I'll sit right here on my porch and I can pickem off." Jud argued with me. "Don't argue with me son. I heard enough. They're comin' here to try and hurt you. I'm not letting it happen."

"None of us are Daniel. You're not going at this alone." Jenna rested her hand on my shoulder and looked up at me. "Now let's get Romeo back."

"What about the wedding?" I asked. I could feel that Romeo was close, and his energy was low. My mind was racing with the thoughts of him dying and it being my fault. "I can't believe Sebastian would do this…"

"It is still early in the day. MaryBell and the staff are handling all of that. Plus, you still have to play at the wedding." Jud gave me a mischievous look and wink at the last part that I returned with a scowl.

"Sebastian would never have sided with the counsel if he had known what they were going to do. He isn't that way. He doesn't ever want someone innocent to suf-" Jenna stopped talking when she realized what she was saying, "I didn't mean it in that way Daniel… you know that…"

"Jenna it is fine… I just need to get Arthur back… get Romeo back. I tried to keep him out of this."

Chester was leaning on the doorframe, "we have company." He said as seven cloaked men appeared at the edge of the ward and fanned out in a line.

Jud raised his rifle, "yer trespassin', I would suggest that you leave that boy with us before I start popping you off one by one."

"There is no need for such violence and certainly not to protect that thing by your side. Hand over the criminal and we won't have any trouble, we will even release the boy." One of the hooded men said calmly with malice behind his voice.

"Thing? Did you really just refer to Daniel as a thing?" Chester started to roll up his sleeves. "Okay, I am ready to rip into someone."

"His name is Merlin. Merlin Pintikelly. A criminal to the crown and to God himself. Anyone that stands with him will also face judgment. Now you can turn him over and receive mercy or you can face execution." It was the same voice from before. It was a voice I even recognized. I had heard it before. A long time ago.

My eyes finally landed on Romeo, and I rushed off the steps minding the ward. "Let him go… he doesn't deserve this."

"Your mother is next Pintikelly if you do not turn yourself in."

"Please, stop… leave everyone alone. I will comply but I must stop Ophelia first. Give me some time…"

"Don't do it Merlin!" I snapped my head around to see Romeo struggling against his bindings and a large man holding him back. "They're working with her! Don't do it!"

"What… how… why would you?"

"To get to you wizard. You have been playing God for far too long, deciding who lives and dies, seducing a divine being to give up their position in Heaven to be with you. Killing royals, even threatening to kill King Wesley. You have also kidnapped his wife and child. Your record isn't becoming of you."

"He didn't kidnap me or my child!" I heard Clara shout from the porch. I could feel the anger coming off her, "and he did not seduce me to leave that godforsaken position as The Bookkeeper for God. I gave it up because I love Merlin. I always have and I always will. Now give me back my brother and get the hell out of here because I am not leaving, and you are not taking Arthur or Merlin anywhere."

I looked back at her and something about her energy shifted and changed. She had a glow to her like she did when she was Vretil.

"Clara…"

"No, I am done having you taken from me over and over again."

A chuckle left the lips of the seven men that stood at the ward line. "Foolish girl. You will continue to meet a horrible fate in every life until you cut ties with him."

"Go to hell." Clara replied.

"Clara, go back inside with Noah. Please." I said to her gently. "I don't want you to get hurt."

"No. Heather has the baby. I am here with you, and I will fight by your side. You just have to let me. Let me be by your side." She stepped off the steps and came over to take my hand in hers. "We are stronger together. We always have been."

"Such a shame, kill the boy." The cloaked man said coldly.

"No!" I shouted and at the same time the gun shots exploded like a thunderclap behind me and I pulled Clara down to the ground. I looked back to see Jud motioning Jenna and Chester to grab Romeo. I hadn't notice that the three had been plotting while the arguing had been going on.

Jenna and Chester were fast. They pulled Romeo away from the large man that was bleeding out with a few more injured. I shouldn't have been shocked. It was rather clear Jud was going to shoot.

"Hmmm no matter. We still have that delicious mother of yours we can get a hold of and why not that little girl you're fond of, Lilith, the littlest Cameron."
"Don't you dare go anywhere near them!"
"You know she is very fond of that little doll you had gotten her last year. Blonde curls like she has with a blue bonnet, blue eyes, and a matching blue dress. Always has it in her arms. Such a bright ten-year-old. It would be a shame if something were to befall her." He sighed and let out a dark laugh.
"Clara get in the house. Now. You need to call Sebastian." I ordered.
"Oh, running to big brother? What can he do?"
"And call the others. They don't understand just who the counsel is." I looked back at the man. "Do they Baal?"
"You figured it out did you peasant? That commoner mind never ceases to amaze me. I still can't see what Vretil sees in you."
"And you are an asshole and that is putting it nicely." I respond dryly.
"Excuse me? You have some nerve... that mouth of yours has always gotten you into trouble. You have never been able to keep it shut and know your place..." Baal replied to me with anger in his voice and behind his eyes.
"Ba- Baal?" Clara stammered out and stumbled back.

"I see you remember me Vretil. Or is it Clara now? What should you be called?" Baal teased her and I placed myself between her and I so his eyes had to stay focused on me.
"Leave her be and everyone else. Your qualm is with me. It always has been." My eyes never left him as I watched him step away from the edge of the ward.

"We are far from done here my dear Merlin. I will see you as close to death as I can make you. Then I will take back what was always meant to be mine. Best be quick, I am sure little Lilith will make you exchange your life much quicker."

We watched them vanish from sight and my blood ran cold. I looked back at Clara and quickly pulled her to me and back to the porch, "Lilith..."
"Chester is taking care of it. He has been on the phone with Sebastian. He is getting her together as fast as he can to get her here." Jenna cut me off.

My mind was racing. This was becoming far more complicated than I had ever thought it could. I held Clara gently in my arms and kissed the top of her head. I could feel her shaking, she was terrified of Baal.

"Good. I will do my best to avoid being around him. I know he…"

"Daniel. That doesn't matter anymore. His little sister's life is at stake and so is Clara's. He won't stay mad if it means keeping them safe." Jenna spoke softly to me and ran her fingers through her short hair. "Are you both okay?"

"I will be fine. Thank you, Jenna. All of you." I looked at her and Jud then to Chester who was leaning on the doorframe now after pressing end to the phone call he had been on with Sebastian.

"I told ya son yer not going at this alone." I felt Jud rest his hand on my shoulder as he spoke to me, "and I know if anyone can do something to stop whatever this mess is that is going on it will be you."

"I hope you're right Judson…" I whispered softly and kissed the top of Clara's head again as she clung to me.

Chapter 7

"Daniel!"

I heard my name get called out from where we had gathered in Jud's study, I looked back seeing Lilith running to me with her baby doll in hand. She flung her arms around my waist and smiled up at me brightly. "Well, hello little one. I see you have your doll with you." I picked her up into my arms. "Yes! And look! We have on matching dresses and our hair in pigtails. See?" Her little face lit up in excitement. She was ten but still always loved to play with her dolls and have tea parties.

"I see that. You both look lovely little one." I looked up to see Sebastian come in behind her. His eyes met mine. They still held hurt and anger behind them, but he didn't make a remark. "Sebastian…"

"Daniel." His response was short. I knew he was still angry. I couldn't very well blame him for that.

"Big brother are you still mad?" Lilith asked in a sad voice to Sebastian. Sebastian let his look soften and he let out a sad sigh, "no Little Bit. I am fine."

She tilted her head and gave him a look and looked between the two of us. "You're a bad liar Bash."

Sebastian let out a heavy sigh and ran his fingers through his hair and looked at me and then to her. "It is complicated Lilith."

"No, it is not."

"Lilith you are too little to understand. "

"No, I am not Bash! You are still blaming him for a choice that Stella made. It isn't his fault."

"Lilith. Yes, it is. Everything that is going on is his fault. It is the results of his actions, and WE are having to pay for it." I could hear the anger building up in his voice.

I set Lilith down out of my arms. "Lilith. Why do you not go find MaryBell. She should be in the kitchen. Just down the hall and through the dining room. The woman giving orders will be who you can probably talk into giving you something sweet to snack on." I said to her and gave her a sad smile. I looked back at Sebastian and then to the others coming back in.

She looked up at me with her big blue eyes that looked sad. Letting out a sad sigh to confirm it, "okay…" She hugged her doll to her and ran out of the room.

Getting back up from where I knelt, I looked back at Sebastian.
"I can feel the tension between you two, but we need to keep things civil. Everything going on is more important right now." Jenna stepped between us with her arms across over her chest.
"Yes, of course. You are right… both of you." I replied softly. "We need to pinpoint where the mass of dark energy is coming from. From there we need to plan accordingly to strike. Seal them away… I just did not account for…"
"That is the thing, isn't it Daniel? You do not think. You have been acting and doing for what will benefit you at the cost of others. Those little stories painting you out to be something else. A hero. A wise old man. Hell even in that damn show that used to come out they painted you as a man of honor and something else completely… but no. You are a coward. A fake. A murderer…"
"Sebastian!" Clara raised her voice to talk over Sebastian. "Just stop… please."
I lowered my eyes and clinched my fists, "no. He is right. This is my fault, and I am so sorry I have pulled you all into this. Your lives are in danger, and it is because of me."
"Daniel…"
"No, Romeo. It is true. I have only ever caused pain and suffering for others… I am the reason why Clara is killed in every life… I am the reason why Camelot fell… I failed you and I have failed her. Over and over again. I am going to fix this… I will set things back into balance and when it is done…"
"Don't you dare say it, Merlin. Don't you dare finish that goddamn sentence." Clara's voice shook slightly as she cut me off. I couldn't meet her eyes. I could feel how broken what I was saying was making her.
"You are not going anywhere. I cannot lose my best friend again." Romeo said to me from where he sat next to Heather as she worked on treating him.
"Here let me heal you." I whispered and walked over to him taking a knee. I held up my hands and a soft golden glow came out and coated him in it. "I am sorry for what they did to you. If I had been there…"
"No, do not blame yourself. You already know I will defend you just as you always have for me." Romeo spoke gently to me and rested his hand on my cheek and looked at me weakly. "It will be an honor to fight by your side

once again. Even if this is our last chance to right a wrong. And you may address me as Arthur."

I chuckled sadly, "oh? Not your Royal Prick?"

He laughed in response and winced clutching his chest. "That smarts…"

I frowned and pushed part of his shirt out of the way. I paled at the black that pooled around his chest attacking his heart. "No…" I swallowed hard and blinked back tears.

"I know I do not have long Merlin. So let us get to work." He pulled his shirt down and gave me a sad smile. "Ophelia cursed me. A little jab at you."

"I- I can fix this… you cannot die Arthur. You said you cannot lose me but here you are dying!" Hot tears started to silently fall, and he gently cleared them off my cheeks. I rested my forehead on his knees and shook my head still trying to fix what Ophelia had done. "You cannot die… please…" His fingers gently played in my hair. He was calm. I could tell he already was facing his death and wasn't scared of it.

"Arthur…" Clara's voice was sad and broken. I knew she was crying without even looking at her. "You won't die. We can fix this. We stop her and it should lift the curse."

"I can't wait to get my hands on that crazy wench." Chester held anger in his voice. "I would never hit a woman but this one… this one I will rip apart."

"We need to pull ourselves together and start planning. We do not have much time." Arthur's voice was calm as he spoke through the pain.

"He is right. If we can get this woman sealed away it may be our only chance at keeping Romeo from dying and stop what is happening." Sebastian finally spoke again after expressing his words against me.

"Daniel," I heard Stellas voice and raised up my head from Arthur's knees to catch sight of her red hair, "Daniel. Pull it together. I understand wanting to break down right now, but they need you. We all need you. Please Daniel."

"She is right you know." Heather said to me and looked at where Stella was standing.

"What is Heather talking about?" Sebastian looked at her confused.

"Heather can see things and hear things… She can see Stella's ghost." Clara whispered and walked to stand with Sebastian.

"Wh- what?" Sebastian paled.

"Tell him to stop being so grumpy and to stop blaming Daniel. It wasn't his fault." Stella said to Heather.

"She said to stop being so grumpy and to stop blaming Daniel for her death."

Sebastian swallowed hard and looked around the room for a hopeful glimpse of her. "Stella…"

"Oh Sebastian… can you tell him I love him? Please."

"She said she loves you Sebastian. She is over here." Heather pointed to where Stella's spirit was.

I watched the hurt coat his face and eyes. "I love you Stella… I am… I should have been with you… I am so sorry."

"It isn't any one's fault. Now everyone needs to get to work. They're running out of time. Look at the battleship that is in the bay. A lot of the spirits are restless they seem to be fleeing from around that area."

"She doesn't want anyone to blame themselves or each other for her death." Heather parroted to everyone. "She wants us to get to work… oh and the big boat in the bay. The one they do history and ghost tours on. She thinks they could be working out of it or near it." Heather tilted her head and looked at Stella, "your energy is stronger than others around here. You have become a spirit guide for Daniel. You aren't a normal ghost."

Stella let out a little laugh and gave a wink at my shocked expression. I wasn't sure how I had missed that, but I did. *'My guide? Why?'*

"Because you need me. Now get to work wizard."

Chapter 8

I walked the length of the room lost in thought with trying to weigh on what to do. I wanted to keep everyone out of this. Learning what I just did changed things drastically. It wasn't just one obsessive vengeful witch we were dealing with, it was so much more and made thing so much worse. The Seven Sages were involved in it and found their way into the Wizard Counsel. They were pulling all the strings. If I had paid closer attention to them then maybe I could have ended them before they awakened.

"Merlin."

I stopped walking back and forth and looked back at the direction of the voice and locked eyes with Arthur.

"You're doing that thing you do when you are worried and you're trying to figure out how to handle it alone. Stop doing that." He said to me as he forced himself to his feet and held his chest.

I moved quickly over to him and held him steady. "Well, I cannot depend on you to not keel over now, can I?"

"Oh, shut it. I will be just fine. I might have a few hints of information that could prove helpful. Maybe. I know you are aware how my family in this life works. How my mum is…"

"You mean the fact that she has been known to use her children to gain information on the royal families and other higher-class families. You sleep with one of them in exchange for money and knowledge. I know she has done things to you herself. You just never speak freely of any of this. I read your mind." I replied with a look of distaste at the images I saw from his mind.

"They do what to you and your siblings?" Clara looked at him with such shock and horror.

"Why didn't you come to one of us or say something sooner? My father could help you three get out of that." Sebastian licked his lips and rubbed his tired eyes. I could tell he hadn't been sleeping well. He pulled a flask from out of his inside suit pocket and unscrewed it to take a large swig.

"I know… it is never easy to come forward and speak out against family. If I did then we would have been pulled from the school and I do not know what would have happened to us after that or even what those higher in

power would have done to us. Not even your father could save us from that Sebastian. Many that are involved are more powerful than him. Down to the judges." He replied and let out a heavy sigh. "But if what I know can help then I want to. Mother sold me to them."

"She sold you!" Chester and Jenna said at the same time. I couldn't believe it myself. Yes, my father in this life is horrible but I would never dream he would do that to me. Then again, he always enjoyed abusing me himself.

"Yes, now can we move on from that? We can come back to it but first we really need to talk about what I learned in the short time being trapped with them. I had sent you a text the other night. Your first night here I believe..." He sighed and leant back on the desk before going on, "I was meant to be at the school, and I was... at first. I went to bed and the next thing I knew I woke up in that same room mother uses for us to..." He grimaced at the words he avoided saying. "Anyways. I was slightly confused and out of it. I felt hands on me and realized what was starting to happen when I fully came awake and heard them. I was being sold off. The man talking was the one you spoke to today. The head of the counsel. They were talking in hushed voices about Celestial objects and needing them. Even though I was in the middle of being... yeah. I kept listening. They said Vretil. I recognized the name. After that your name was pulled into the conversation and they brought up the dagger Sompero. It has been remade down to the exact one you have. They plan to use it on you. Which you figured that out. How they got your spell I do not know but they did. They want to use your powers to limit magick more than it already is."

"They already tried one time back in the 1800's when they killed Sophia." Clara chimes in. "How did they even get their hands on the spell to make a copy of your dagger?" I could see the frantic fear in her eyes as she took my arm.

"Yes, but I cheated on my end to make sure nothing would be limited to what they wanted, and everyone can do magick just as they can now. It is not as powerful as it used to be for you all... but they lied to me as well. They killed you... killed Sophia. Used her as the sacrifice when you were promised to be released to me... I failed you then and so many other times... I am sorry." I swallowed hard and ran my fingers through my hair and avoided her sad eyes, but she only gently turned my cheek to look down at her. She leaned up and gently kissed my lips and wrapped her arms around me to rest her head on my chest. I held her to me and took in her scent and worked to calm my racing mind, "The only thing I can think of was Ophelia must have gotten hold of it during one of the many times she would welcome herself into my chambers. I put everything away that was of importance. Hid them… at least I thought I did."

"Could it be that they had time to study it before you got the original copy back from them during the time you got captured a couple of years ago?" I looked up to see Argon come in with the other three immortals and Argon's son Callen.

"Argon? What are you doing here?" Sebastian questioned in concern.

"We came to help of course, but do you think that could be possible as well Merlin," Argon averted his attention back to his question. "Do you think they could have had time to study it then?"

"It is possible but just as those chains that I should have had the only spell, but they managed to get their hands on them."

"Regardless of how they got them, we need to know what to do now to stop them from using those things on you. They plan to pull from your energy. The life crystal that is inside you. If they get their hands on you again, we may not be able to get you back." Arthur looked at me with worry in his eyes regardless of how he was feeling for himself. "I heard whispers of where they plan to hold you, but I am not completely sure. The drugs started to make it hard to concentrate. I know it will be underground."

"We may have the upper hand here." Jenna chimes in from where she was leaning on the wall. "Do they know you heard them at all talking?"

"No, not that I am aware of. I kept up the act of… never mind. No. I do not believe so."

"Then this could help us. Do you have a counter for those objects that you created?"

I gave her a nod and licked my lips. "Yes, but you still have to be so close to cast it."

"We can handle that. They are not the only ones with power on their side." Agate looked at his nails then back at us with a little smirk on his lips.

"Very good point. Plus, we have a little help in the waters which if they are on the big boat… my kind have been known to handle larger crafts than that. No one is immune to the songs of the water." Citrine had a mischievous smile on her face as if she had missed causing trouble to sailors like she used to, and honestly, she probably did but I was not one to comment against it considering the trouble I cause on my own.

"Let us not sink that ship. It is a historical monument, but you can use that beautiful voice of yours to handle things how you used to just as your kids can do as well. I think they are overdue for a snack." Argon tilted her chin up to look at the water elemental. She had a slight pout to her lips but that vanished quickly and turned into a blush when she looked into his eyes, "be a good girl and maybe I will treat you later when we are alone."

I rolled my eyes and shook my head.

"Honestly father. Save the bedroom talk for later. We have stressing matters at hand."

"This is just a little motivation Callen. Stop being so uptight. I swear you sound like Merlin."

"I am most certainly not "uptight" I just do not display my kinks so openly your majesty. I prefer to have class about myself."

Argon chuckled at my scowl and held up his hands in defeat.

I sigh and shake my head, "but yes. I can break the spells on what they have. It will require me getting close to them. With all your added help it should make it less of a challenge. The problem still rests on the matter of Ophelia. We cannot underestimate her. More than likely she will have brought Thomas and Areses back and if they are back then the other horrible things that Areses spawns are back as well."

"Are you sure? We do not need the added... never mind." Chester rubbed the back of his neck and let out a heavy sigh taking a seat next to Heather and pulling her into his lap.

Rubbing my tired eyes, I could feel the stress weighing down on me. Time was ticking and we were running out of time to stop what was happening. Governments from all over the globe were doing everything to cover up what was actually happening. If anyone found out what was really going on than there would be an uprising. What better way to control mass amounts of people than putting fear in them from wars and recessions? Separate them and divide nations, pin brother against brother, turning many against one another while the governments continue to pour fuel on the flames to keep its people under their thumbs. "I am sure of it Chester. With everything going on it would only give to reason why this world is going to hell more and more. Dark forces are at play. It is worse than anyone outside of us would be able to understand. We have to stop it."

"So, what is the plan, Merlin? How soon are we setting out?" Argon questioned me.

"Citrine, have your children scout out the location. Have them find the best point in entry on the ship if that is where a lot of the energy is coming from. If not, find out. Then report back to us. They are our eyes and ears right now."

"Until then we have a wedding to help with. We busy ourselves and not let on that we know more than they want us to." Clara took my hand in hers and looked up at me. "You are not getting out of this."

I sighed heavily and shook my head. "Clearly."

"I do not want attitude from you Merlin. This is keeping you safe and close to me for as long as possible. I know you always promise to come back to me, and you do... but I fear the day when one day you don't or cannot... I don't want that to happen. To see you only as a ghost. To not get to be physically in your arms and left still with an emptiness, because Merlin you are my home and without you..."

I pulled her into my arms and held her tightly to me. My chest felt tight. "Please don't let what is happening cost me you... not again." She whispered into my chest.

"I promise Princess."

"Come on. We all should get cleaned up for tonight. We can all help. Plus, it gives extra security if they decide to attack." Arthur said and pushed slightly off the desk he was leaning back on. His complexion was pale, and I could tell he was in pain. What I did only slowed down the effects of the curse. It didn't break it.

Chapter 9

Chattering from the wedding with guests coming in echoed around the property. Their chatter mixed with the soft symphony of Clara's violin. Chester managed to talk Sebastian to take my place behind the piano. I held Noah and watched Sebastian's fingers dance along the keys as the siblings harmonized together naturally.

"They're really good." MaryBell came up to me and playfully pinched Noah's cheeks.

"Yes, they are. They have practiced and done concerts together from the time they were small children."

Noah giggled as MaryBell played with him, "Well, I can tell she is a keeper."

"She has to be to put up with this one." Jud came up and nudged my arm with a mischievous smile on his face.

Rubbing my arm, I let out a sad laugh, "she is special. I am very lucky that in each life she still chooses to be with me."

"When all this is over you should pop the question." Jud whispers to me as everything gets quiet and they start the ceremony.

The outdoor venue was decorated in a rustic fashion. Rows of white wooden foldout chairs lined on each side with guests for the couple. Lanterns lit the way down to the altar where the groom stood nervously waiting for his bride to come out and walk down to him. Fairy lights hung with the white curtains that were pulled back that he stood under. He kept looking back at the pastor that held an amused understanding look on his face. I watched the old man talk softly to him. Sebastian switched up the keys and all eyes turned to the bride's maids and the groom's men that walked ahead before the bride. I let my eyes linger over to Clara that followed her brothers' lead. Her fingers moved gracefully over the strings as her bow moved smoothly with it. Her eyes briefly locked on to mine and I saw the sadness in them.

'Do you remember how I asked you to marry me back then?' I asked her, letting my mind link on to hers. I watched her close her eyes and gave a sad nod.

'Yes, you took me to our spot in a small clearing in the woods outside the castle. The only place we never got bothered. It was our secret. Like so many others.'

The flower girl started down the walkway and the pastor motioned for everyone that was sat to stand for the bride that stood with her father. All eyes were on her in her ivory lace gown. I watched the groom come to tears. His eyes never leaving his lovers face. They joy I felt from him was easy for everyone to see. The girl's father held out his arm for her to take and they moved slowly down the isle. The young bride worked to hold back her own tears and smiled happily through them.

"I was leaning on one of the large old trees. The wildflowers had started to bloom. You had wanted to pick some of them. You were in my arms playing with the bright petals of the spring flowers. You were sad though. Because you had taken a thrashing from Uther the day before when you had come back from a mission. I had gone out to greet you. I was excited to see you. I had missed you... I kissed you and he saw... I was jerked away from you. He took the horse whip..."

"Yes... I remember."

"I begged him to stop... but he didn't. Arthur heard my screaming and rushed from the stables and put a stop to it. You didn't react though. You held it in. Uther hated that."

"He hated me regardless. No matter what he did to me it was never enough to keep me from you. The next morning, I asked your chamber maid to tell you to meet me in our spot, and you did. I watched you pick the flowers till I pulled you to me so I could hold you. I could tell you were still upset over what had happened. I kissed you."

"Then you moved away from me and got down on one knee keeping hold of my hand. I was confused but I quickly understood... you slipped a ring on my finger. It was an amethyst on a silver band. You asked me to marry you and I quickly said yes and dropped to my knees, and I kissed you."

I watched Clara as tears rolled down her cheeks and she locked her eyes back on to mine.

"You may now kiss the bride." I broke my thought at the words of the pastor and the cheering from the friends and family of the happy couple. Noah was in my arms clapping his little hands just as the others around us had been doing. He looked up at me with excited eyes at the wonders around us taking it all in. I couldn't help but let a laugh leave me. Lilith came running up to me with her doll in hand both wearing matching dresses and their hair in pigtails.

"Daniel! Daniel!" Her eyes held excitement and chocolate around her mouth.

"What is it little one?"

"They have a chocolate fountain!"

"Is that so?" I chuckled, "I wasn't aware." I pulled out my handkerchief and knelt to clean her mouth. "Are you supposed to be eating sweeties this late?"

"Shhh don't tell Bash or Clara!" She held her finger up to her lips and giggled.

"It will be our little secret."

She quickly hugged my neck and kissed my cheek before she ran off when she spotted Chester walking past with a plate full of food.

"I think it is time to feed you as well Noah. Are you hungry?"

"Yes."

I looked at him shocked and he only laughed. "You can talk?"

"Just because I am a baby it doesn't mean I can't talk. Just no one listens. It is easier with you."

"This is a new one, does your mother know you can do this little trick?"

"No. Lilith does."

"I see." I walked us back up to the house to feed and change him to get him ready for bed. "You know you cannot keep calling me daddy. I am not..." I sighed and looked down at the little boy that sat on my bed at this point after he was changed into his pajamas and fed he started playing with Amethyst that came out to visit him.

He looked back at me with his big blue eyes that matched Clara's, *"yes I can. You are my daddy also."*

"I cannot believe I am having a conversation with a baby." I mumbled and sat on the bed with them.

"I can hear you father."

I pinched the bridge of my nose and let out a heavy sigh, "if anything, you have my personality, and I don't know if that is a good thing. You are a clever little thing."

He smiled up at me and crawled over to me letting out a sleepy yawn. Plopping down on me he stuck his thumb in his mouth and closed his eyes. gently stroked his curly blonde hair as he slept on me.

I closed my eyes and rested my head back on the pillow with my mind racing from the day's events.

"There you two are."

I blinked my eyes open seeing Clara smiling down at us from where she came and sat on the bed.

"Is the wedding over?"

"Yes. Did you even eat? You didn't stay for the reception."

"No, I forgot. I was distracted." I whispered and nod to Noah. "He can talk."

"Well yes, he knows basic words like he should."

"No, he can actually talk. Have a conversation with me using my little trick like did with you earlier."

Her mouth dropped open, and she looked between the two of us in shock.

"I was shocked as well."

"How is that possible?"

"I am not sure. Very few have that ability if any. Unless someone or I make a connection for it to be able to happen. I did not make one. He did it himself. Clever little child. You have your hands full with this one when he can actually talk and get around."

"So, he is definitely your child is what I am hearing." She teased.

I laughed softly and ran my fingers through my hair and shrugged in response.

"I am going to get ready for bed. Do you want me to put him in the crib?"

"No. He is fine. Plus, Amethyst seems to like having him to cuddle up with." I nodded to the sleeping dragon that had taken up a place to sleep nuzzled into Noah and me.

She smiled thoughtfully down at them and looked back at me, "I love you, Merlin." She leaned over to me and kissed my lips softly.

"And I you, my Princess." I whispered back to her. "Do you wish me to run you a bath?"

"No, I am tired. I can take one in the morning but thank you. I will be quick. You are still dressed as well. I won't take long so you can get changed and comfortable."

"No need to rush. I am fine." I gave her hand a gently squeeze. "Plus, he has made me his pillow, so I am held hostage by an adorable tiny mage."

She covered her mouth to muffle her laughter. Shaking her head in amusement she got up from where she was sat on the bed. "Then I will arrange your ransom for your release come morning."

"I believe his ransom consists of a bottle and hugs from his mother." I teased.

"You are ridiculous. Adorable, but ridiculous." She sighed and worked to undress herself to get changed.

My eyes lingered over her curves and up to lock eyes back onto hers when she caught me looking. "Sorry." I looked away and bit my lower lip.

"Why are you sorry?"

"It was rude of me."

"You are very much a gentleman. It is adorable."

After twenty minutes she slipped under the covers and nuzzled into bed with us. I kissed the top of her head and then her lips. "Get some sleep."

"You will be here in the morning, right?"

"I promise."

"Good."

I felt her cling to my dress shirt not letting me go as she drifted off. I looked down at her sleeping. It saddened me. I knew how scared she was and honestly, I was terrified as well. I closed my eyes and let out a heavy sigh working myself to go back to sleep.

Chapter 10

Crying pulled me out of my slumber. I leaned up slightly and looked over at Clara fighting in her sleep sobbing. She called out my name. I shifted Noah off me gently and I moved to pull Clara to me working to calm her down. "Clara... Clara wake up. It is okay. You are only dream..." I furrowed my brow at seeing her dream. It wasn't a dream. She was seeing what the future could be. I swallowed hard and let out a shaky breath. "Clara..." Her eyes popped open, and she flung her arms around me and cried heavily into my neck. "Shh I am right here. I won't let it happen." The image replayed in my mind. It was only flashes of what could come but it still sickened me. I was forced to me knees with my hands cuffed behind me and Ophelia standing over with the dagger in hand. She plunged it into my chest. "I won't let that happen... I promise..."
Clara kept crying and stayed clung to me as I rocked her in my arms. I looked up to see Stella looking down at us sadly.
A soft knock came to the door, "who is it?" I questioned.

"It's Jenna. Citrine has news. She said she will let us know what she has learned at breakfast."
"Okay, give us a moment and we will be down."
"Of course."
I heard her walk away and I looked down at Clara who was working to calm herself down. Her breathing was shaky just as she shook in my arms. "Please. Please do not go. Please. Please Merlin... please. Please don't leave me... please."
She looked up at me with sad blue eyes that were puffy and red from her crying. "Clara I..."
"No... no don't say it just don't... Please Merlin!"
Noah started to cry, making Clara jump and stop talking. She shifted her attention to Noah as she pulled him into her arms, "I am sorry. Shh mummy has you. *Lavenders blue dilly dilly Lavenders green when you walk in dilly dilly I shall be queen.*" She softly sang to him calming him with the lullaby.
"I am going to get changed..." I said gently and moved from off the bed. She only gave me a nod and avoided my eyes. "Clara, I do not have a choice. I must do this. I must stop them."

"Just go change Merlin." She didn't look at me and her voice held a mix of anger and sadness in it when he spoke to me.

I lowered my eyes and gave her a slight bow before excusing myself. We spent the next twenty to thirty minutes not talking and getting ready for the day. She was upset. I understood and as much as I didn't want to have to face what we were having to face I knew it had to be done because things were only getting worse. I had to do something to stop the threat. I held the door open for her to go through first and I closed it behind us.

We found the others already in the dining room with Tiffany serving them. Her eyes quickly locked on to me and a little smirk rested on her lips as her eyes lingered over me. I rolled my eyes and pulled a chair out for Clara to sit before I sat next to her.

"Good morning handsome, let me guess, tea with the milk on the side." I heard Tiffany say behind me in an all too friendly voice and ran a hand along my shoulder and slightly played with my hair.

"It is only proper for the lady to get her order first or do you just fancy flirting with someone that is already committed to another?" I looked up at her giving her a cold look. "And take your hand off me."

"Oop. Well, it seems you have made em cranky." Chester grinned a mischievous grin and looked between us.

Tiffany narrowed her eyes at me and gave Clara a hateful look and then looked back at me removing her hand from where it was on my shoulder. "Sorry. What can I do for you little friend then?"

Sebastian arched a brow and cleared his throat. "Actually, you can go get another serve for us or asked the owners to come out. I am sure they would enjoy hearing how you are treating their guest. You will not be speaking to my sister like that or treating her partner the way you are."

I was surprised to hear Sebastian speak on my behalf.

Tiffany gave a sound of frustration and stormed off into the kitchen.

"What is her problem?" Jenna questioned.

"Jealousy. Anyways, Citrine. You have news?" I say and glance next to me at Clara busying herself with Noah.

"What's goin' on? Tiffany came into the kitchen in tears." Jud walked up cutting Citrine off from talking.

I rubbed my eyes and let out an annoyed sigh. "Your little waitress is rude and disrespectful. She was simply put in her place."

Jud sighs and shakes his head. "Are ya two wanting what you had yesterday just the tea how you had it the other day?" He asked me.

"Clara?" I say her name gently and she gave a nod. "Yes please. Thank you, Judson."

Judson gave a nod and went back into the kitchen. I moved my attention back on Citrine who took in a deep breath and shook her head. "It is a mess on that ship with all the dark energy. It is bad. Annalisia found out they have a portal that is between here and somewhere to Ireland. She kept hearing them say The Hollow. Does that mean anything to you?"

I shook my head. "No, but it was in Ireland that they sacrificed Sophia. It could be linked to that. Did she go through the portal?"

"No, I was not sure if she would be safe to do that. From listening to the ones on the vessel talking she found out that the magical items they created based off yours is in the lower level of the ship. She said it sounds like they have created a holding cell. That is also where the portal is. The objects are guarded heavily."

I rubbed my chin in thought, working over everything and what would be best to do.

"Citrine, have your children start working on putting many on the ship in whatever hypnotic state you use and get them into the water? It will lessen the forces against us." Arthur interjected cutting off my thoughts.

"What about those that are innocent that did not want this?" Heather questioned. Worry coated her voice that matched her expression, "can they not be spared?"

"Heather, it is not that simple. This is war. Casualties will happen. We have already seen plenty of that at Prospero. Children as young as eight have lost their lives because of this. It will not be easy to avoid. If it can work that we can save and free those then we will. Aside from that I cannot promise those that are forced to stand with her will not be killed, either by one of us or by Citrine's children." Arthur said gently but in a firm voice. I could tell it pained him to say that. He never wanted war even when he ruled over Camelot, but he still picked up his sword and fought. "I am sorry Heather. It is how things have to be."

Heather lowered her eyes and Chester pulled her to him and she rested her head on his shoulder.

Jud came out with the order for Clara and I and sat it down for us.

"Thank you, Judson."

"Yer welcome son. Tiffany won't be botherin' y'all anytime soon. She is on wash duty."

"Delightful." I replied and took to fixing Clara's tea how she took hers and then I fixed mine.

"Here, let me see little man so y'all can eat. Maybe we can go sneak somethin' sweet."

"Can I come?" Lilith chimes in and scrambles off her chair from where she was sat next to Sebastian.

"Lilith, you should not be running around. They still have work to do." Sebastian scolds.

"But Bash…"

"Lilith." He shakes his head.

"Ah she won't be botherin' us. We raised a house full of kids and grandbabies. I think we can manage these two. Plus, you can help Nannie do some cookin'. Do you like to cook?" Jud held his hand out for Lilith to take and she quickly took it and gave an excited nod in response.

Lilith looked back at her brother and stuck out her tongue at him. I covered my mouth to muffle a laugh he gave a hateful look in response to.

"Sorry." I chuckled, "she is an amusing child. She has spark in her."

"Yes, but she has learned some bad habits in defiance and back talking in school. I wonder who she learned that from?" I could tell it was more of a statement than a question and it was a jab at me.

I shrugged and took a sip of tea, "they are a bunch of idiots. At least I have given her proper lessons. Anyways. Continue Arthur." I nod to my king to go on while I took another sip of tea.

Arthur rubs his temples and winces at the pain from his chest. "We move out tonight. Agate and Citrine can create a fog to cover us. With Argon's children we will be able to have eyes to move through it to sneak onboard. We shouldn't teleport onto the ship. That would be expected. With the storm coming through tonight we can use the storm and fog as coverage. We will have to move quick and swiftly. Merlin, we will need you and Sebastian to get along well enough to create a proper shield for each group. You both are our strongest when it comes to casting aside from Clara. She will not be joining us. I want her, Heather, and Jenna to stay here with Carnelian. They will be here to hold things down and to receive the injured. Both Heather and Clara are skilled at that and aside from that the immortal blood from Carnelian will aid in speeding things along. Fresh water and linen will be needed if we are able to save any that are innocent in all of this like Mark and his friends had been. I never encountered him, but I do remember what Merlin told me had happened. I know many are innocent and we will not be able to save them all when we have the whole world of innocence to think of."

Silence sat over the table for longer than I would like to say. The clanking and scraping from utensils to cups could only be heard.

"We will be ready to go at night fall." I finally broke the silence and sat my teacup down on the saucer.

"So that's it? You just get to decide?" Clara said in cold tone of voice.

"Clara…" Arthur tried to speak.

"No." Clara pushed herself up from her chair and I took her hand but she jerked it away from me. "No, you both always… always leave me. You both know I can fight, and I should be by your side." She steps away from the table in frustration and slightly stumbles and starts to pale.

"Clara?" I got up quickly and caught her in my arms. "Clara!"

"What happened?" Sebastian moved around the table and came to her side. Agate picked up her teacup and sniffed it before taking a small taste. "She has been poisoned."

"What? How? None of them could have gotten in." I looked at him in shock and confusion. I had fixed her tea. I didn't smell or notice anything out of the ordinary. I missed it. "This is my fault. How did I miss that?" I held her to me and kept my hand placed over her chest healing her.

"Let me see the cup." Callen took the cup from Agate holding his hand over it. "Veneum Reamorva Acteum." The elf chanted. Pulling from the cup was the substance used to poison Clara. "Witch-hazel."

"Witch-hazel?" Chester questioned.

"Yes. It is used for many things but overly consumed it is a silent poison. Slowly shuts the body down. Easy enough to pass and blend with tea." Callen explained, "someone has been feeding her this since she has been here and possibly before then. I cannot be sure." He lowered his hand and the substance dropped back into the teacup.

Color slowly returned to her, and a pained moan left her lips.

"Clara?" I whispered her name and cupped her cheek.

She moved her hand to her head, "what happened?" Her eyes fluttered open and looked up at me confused, catching the worry written all over my face.

"You have been getting poisoned." Sebastian said to her gently.

"Why only target her?" Carnelian questioned.

Sebastian and I helped Clara get to her feet slowly, but she stayed gripped on to me.

"To make a point that no matter what, none of us are safe and they have ways to get in. This also means a spy is in this building." Argon chimes in from where he stayed sat at the table.

Arthur ran his fingers through his long blonde hair that was almost white that he had pulled back loosely, "we need to question Tiffany. I have a feeling she is behind it."

"How could I have been kept from reading her thoughts?" I questioned.

"Or any of us. She seems to have a way to block it out." Agate eyed the kitchen. "Time to bring her out and ask a few questions." He said coldly.

"I think she will talk more one on one. I will do it. She fancies me for a reason so let's find out why." I let Sebastian take Clara who gripped my hand. I looked back at her, and she shook her head. "I will be fine Clara." I brought her hand to my lips and kissed it gently.

"No, let someone else do it."

"She won't talk to the others. She has taken a strong liking to me from the time I stepped foot into the place. Let me go."

"Clara. He is right." Jenna took her hands and gave her a gentle look.

"Plus, he won't be alone. Take a walk in the garden. Callen can blend in, and I can have a listen from blending in as well." Argon nods for me to go on.

"Thank you." I looked back at Clara and give her a gentle look before giving a slight bow and departing into the kitchen.

Tiffany looked up from where she sat on the counter and gave me a smirk, "if it isn't the pretty boy. What do you need?"

"You and I need to have a talk, Tiffany. Fancy a walk so we can talk this over?"

She looked me over with an amused smile and got off the counter. "Sure. Lead the way."

I nod for her to follow me out to the garden. I was silent for a moment picking up on where Argon and Callen had placed themselves.

"Well?" Tiffany pulled me from my thoughts.

"Right, why have you been acting so harshly? When I first got here you had a different attitude. As if by overnight your mood changed. Why is that?"

She giggled a flirty laugh, "because I have a crush on you. You can't get better than someone who is already married."

"How did you know she was married?"

"She is in magazines. Their wedding was even shown on the TV."

"I see. So, you think that is a reason to mistreat her? She never wanted to be married to him. Her and I are in love and always have been."

"We all have a first love, but it doesn't mean you stay with them or put up with them. I mean she is cheating on her husband with you. That means she would also cheat on you with someone."

"It is not like that, and you know it."

"What do you mean?"

"I am done playing nice. Why did you poison Clara?"

She stopped walking and looked at me. Her flirty demeanor shifted, and a look of malice took its place. "You really are just as clever as they say. I take it you were able to cure her quickly. They say your skills are unmatched." She walked around me letting her fingers trail over my shoulders till she came back around to face me and ran her fingers along the buttons to my blue button down that already had a few undone. Her eyes lingered over the amethyst that hung around my neck then looked back up at me. "Merlin."

I glared down at her and moved her hands from touching me any further with how low she was letting them try to travel. "I told you before to keep your hands off me. So, because you know who I am you wanted to kill Clara?"

"Oh no, we knew she would not die. You would save her. We need her alive because she will be the key in making sure all of this works for the Mistress. Although, she wants to keep you as her own personal toy. I cannot say I blame her. You are wonderful to look at dressed and undressed. Well, from what I have heard on the undressed part."

I crossed my arms over my chest and glared at her, "why is Clara the key? If Ophelia gets her hands on me then why would she need Clara?"

"Clara is a very powerful witch. Well, not completely a witch. She is still very much an angel. A divine person. Her blood and power that can be pulled from her would ensure just what Mistress wants to happen." She looked at me in amusement while she chewed on her lower lip.

"I see, so why can I not read your mind?"

"Secrets." She puts a finger to her lips and turned on her heels. "If we are done here and I am not going to win more from you than a chat I really need to get back to work." She gave a slight wave and excused herself from the conversation.

Argon and Callen came to stand next to me.

"We will need to keep a closer eye on Clara. She has to stay here in these wards for her own safety." Callen says in a worried voice.

"Yes, it seems so. I feel like she left a few things out." Argon looked down at me from where he was standing.

"I think you are right. She told us things but didn't at the same time.

"We need to talk to the others." Argon started to walk back to the inn nodding for us to follow him.

Chapter 11

"So, she is working for Ophelia? She doesn't have powers but what is keeping her from not staying on the other side of the ward?" Jenna questioned from where she sat behind Jud's desk with her feet propped up, her sleeves rolled up from her shirt showing off her arms that she had tattoos on.

"When I created the ward, I had it done up to keep out the dark magick and those tainted with it from being turned. She is not either of those. She is just a mortal with no magick. A normal human that can pass freely in and out of here." I replied and leaned up against one of the large bookshelves behind me. "We are going to have to be a lot more careful with what we say and whom we talk around."

"And careful with what we eat and drink." Sebastian adds on.

"Should we not inform Judson and MaryBell?" Heather was sat with Chester playing with his fingers while she spoke. "Shouldn't they know?"

I licked my lips. I was still wondering on that. I had yet to decide. I felt it was safer the less they knew but at the same time the more they knew might save them. "We will, not while Tiffany is here though. I am not sure what she could or would do and I do not want to risk her hurting them out of anger."

"Right, of course." A frown crossed Heather's face as she wrapped her arms around Chester for comfort, "and you better be careful tonight and come home to me." She poked his nose gently.

Chester chuckled in response and kissed her finger she had poked him with and then kissed her lips tenderly, "I promise I will be safe and come back to you."

"You said Tiffany called Clara the key? Do you know what she meant by that?" Sebastian took a swig from his flask before screwing the lid back on, putting it away, pulling out his cigarette case and lighting one.

Letting out a heavy sigh I ran my fingers through my dark hair, "I am not sure. She did not go into detail, but she said enough that I know it is not good."

"Basically, they want my angel blood for what they plan to do and that will more than likely require me to become immortal again." Clara took her place next to me and rested her head on my arm.

I pulled her in and let her rest her head on my chest instead and a sick feeling washed over me. "Exchanging my immortality for yours. Taking mine to restore yours."

"But what about your life crystal?" Arthur questioned.

"I don't know. Regardless of that I do not want to find out just what their plan is. I want to stop them before they get that chance."

"Of course. Are you sure you can break the enchantment of those objects before anything goes wrong? We will still have to get them sealed away again."

"I am going to have to. If not... I do not know when we will get the chance again or if we will even get that chance again. We have one shot, and this plan has to work for it."

Arthur gave me a look of worry with weak eyes from the curse eating away slowly at him, "I believe in you Merlin. If anyone can fix this it, will be you."

I wish I could believe in myself the way him and the others believed in me, but I didn't. "Right, let's get to work on making the objects to enchant and seal them away in. We will not be able to do what was done before." With a flick of my wrist one of my books rested in my hand. I flipped it open and thumbed through the pages that Clara skimmed over with me. I smiled down at her and kissed the top of her head while I searched for what would be needed.

"What are you thinking?" Clara asked me in a whisper.

"I am thinking I am going to change what I have done in a spell before. This time they will all be sealed away in a book. Each page dedicated to each of them. Including doing the same to each member of the Seven Sages. If they are sealed away, then they will not be able to reincarnate. Trap them."

"That is brilliant!" Her face lit up and she pulled away from me slightly. "We would be free of them permanently."

I looked at the others that listened in on the conversation. "It is the best option I can come up with."

"It sounds like a better idea than any right now. What will you do with the book after?" Argon questioned.

"Have it buried on sacred ground maybe. I have yet to think that far ahead."

"Fair enough."

The sound of thunder rolling in gave way to the storm brewing outside. Chills coated my body as the rain poured down over the inn. I looked at my watch and it was a quarter past six.

"It is almost time." Sebastian said softly.

"This is my last chance." I whispered and pulled Clara closer into me and nuzzled into her blonde locks. "I am not letting them get their hands on you again. I will do everything in my power to protect you."

"Do we remember the plan?" Arthur asked as he looked the room over. Excalibur was strapped at his waist where it sat comfortably with his arm rested on it.

"Yes, I believe we all do." Agate gave Arthur a nod, "I will get some control over the weather to help us move better in the dark."

"Excellent. At ten we move out. The streets have less traffic on them to put anyone else in danger." Arthur spoke in a calm firm voice. I could still see the king in him that he has always been. He was a leader again and one I would still always gladly serve under.

Separating from the others I closed the door to my room behind me and locked it. Walking over to Clara I sat on the bed next to her, tucking strands of hair behind her ear before leaning in to kiss her deeply. She laid back on the bed pulling me down to her tangling her fingers in my hair. Parting from her slightly I whispered on her lips, "I love you. More than I could ever express. I promise I will always, and forever be yours and come back to you. Nothing will keep me from you." Silent tears escaped me that she gently cleaned away. "I am sorry. Forgive me." I sat up and rubbed my hands over my eyes cleaning the tears away.

She sat up and hugged me around my waist and kissed my neck. "You have nothing to be sorry for. I know you are more scared than you are letting on. It is okay to be scared Merlin." Her voice was soft as she spoke to me.

"Why do you put up with me? I have brought you nothing but grief in each life. I am not good for you."

"Because I am and always will be in love with you Merlin. I could never see myself with anyone else but you. You are not what has led to my downfall, it has been what we are still fighting against today. It is those hungry for power and fueled by jealousy."

I looked down into her blue eyes and gave her a sad smile, "I truly am a lucky man to have you by my side in each life that you have lived."

"We will always find our way back to each other. Always." She pulled me to lay back down with her. She traced a spot on my chest and looked up at me. "Do you still have the tattoo on your chest that you used to have hidden by magick?"

"Yes."

"Why do you still hide it?"

I shrugged and unbuttoned my shirt and pulled it off. Slowly the magick melted away to reveal the marking. The Triquetra. Her fingers traced the beautiful tattoo that I always hid from others during our time in Camelot. The black ink still looked fresh as if I had just gotten it.

"You do not have to hide it anymore. It is more accepted now." She gently planted kisses over the Triquetra and then up to my neck.

I closed my eyes taking in each feeling of her lips on my skin before I tilted her chin up to lock my lips on to hers. I moved to shift her onto her back as I continued to kiss her. If this was going to be the last time, I get to see her then I was going to make the most of this moment together. I trailed my hand up her leg pushing back the burgundy fabric of skirt of the dress while she unbuckled my belt and unbuttoned my grey slacks pushing the fabric away. I removed them the rest of the way. Slowly I removed her clothes. Trailing my fingers gently over her skin taking in every inch of her curves and places she found as imperfections but for me it showed the beauty of her giving life to another.

Tangled under the sheets I gently eased myself in her as she pulled me to her to kiss me deeply with tears silently rolling down her cheeks. I could make love to her for hours and that was what I planned to do until I had to leave. She wrapped her legs around me to pull me in more to her while I thrusted in and out of her. Her soft moans muffled by my lips deeply kissing hers. The feel of her nails raking down my back as she started to trail kisses along my jaw line and down to my neck. I closed my eyes savoring every moment of it.

Whispering into my ear, "I love you, Merlin."

I moved to place her to straddle me while I thrusted up into her. I traced her lower lip with my thumb and investigated her cerulean blues, "and I love you." With the same thumb I cleaned tears away from her cheeks that escaped her eyes. "Do you wish me to stop?"

She shook her head, "no."

Rolling her hips over mine I took in a sharp breath of pleasure and let out a moan against her skin that coated in chills when I kissed along it moving to her breasts. I took each nipple in turn teasing them with my teeth and tongue, her pace never letting up as she moved her hips over mine. The feel of her walls tightening over my member gave way to her climax. I removed her hands from her mouth that she tried to cover to hide her loud moans and

pinned them behind her back. Her cheeks flushed over at my actions that made me smirk.

"Why try to hide them? I want to hear just how I affect you."

She chewed on her lower lip as moans escaped her. Her cheeks staying tinted over my words and actions.

"Hmm Princess?" I teased and watched her expression as she continued to try and suppress each loud moan while she hit her climaxes.

"I- I don't want anyone to hear me." Her cheeks turned to a brighter shade of pink, and she started to breathe heavily with her moans mixing in. She struggled against my hold on her that only made her walls tighten more around me. Whimpers of pleasure passed her lips as I thrusted up into her. Laying her back on the bed I moved to pin her wrist above her head with one hand and the other to rub over her sensitive area making her squirm under me. The sound of my name rolling off her tongue mixed in with her moans drove me more. I felt myself throbbing in her as sweat beaded along my skin mixing with hers. With one last thrust I finished in her.

Rolling off her I pulled her close to me and kissed her lips deeply. My heart pounded loudly in my chest. I laid my head back on the pillow closing my eyes with her head rested on my chest. Looking at my watch I frowned at the time and let out a heavy sigh and a shaky breath.

"You are about to have to go, aren't you?"

"Yes…"

"Promise me Merlin; promise me that you will come back to me."

"I promise Princess, I will always come back to you." I felt like I was saying it more for myself than for her and honestly, I was. I kissed her fingers gently before slipping off the bed to get dressed.

She sat up on the bed with the sheets pulled up over her chest. I could tell she was trying to hold it together and not plead with me to stay.

I pulled on my black button down and black slacks and belt. I looked back at her and gave her a sad smile. "Do not look so worried. I will see you come morning light."

"It is hard to not… part of me wants to order you to stay but that would be selfish of me." She said to me as I slipped on my black Oxfords.

"Trust me, I will and am coming back to you." I leant down and kissed her deeply. "Stay safe here."

A knock came to the door, "it is time to go." Arthur's voice sounded from the other side of the door.

I looked back at Clara and took in one last look at her before kissing her again, "I love you with every fiber of my being. You are my light."

"I love you, Merlin." She choked back a sob and flung her arms around me to hug me tightly to her. I held her in my arms and rocked her while she cried into my neck.

"Merlin, we need to go. I am sorry to break up the moment." Arthur's voice sounded from the other side of the door.

I reluctantly pulled away from her and looked at her sadly. The rain was beating heavily on the windows as the thunder rolled outside like a fierce battle. Her tear-filled eyes looked me over one last time before I left the room to join Arthur. I closed the door behind me and heard a loud sob break from her. I swallowed back a sob of my own. Locking eyes on Arthur that held a sad look he nodded for me to follow him.

"I truly am sorry. I wish there was another way."

"As do I." I let out a shaky breath to calm my nerves. Catching sight of red hair Stella came into focus. *'Stella.'*

"You have to keep your head on straight tonight, Merlin."

'I know.'

"Then focus."

I sighed and rolled my eyes at her words. Reaching the bottom step, I looked everyone over, "let's get this over with." I tell them.

Agate managed to calm the storm that raged on around us. The waves crashed against the shore and docks. Nearing the large ship, waves of large dark energy flooded off it. The large military vessel rocked in the waves. Dim lights lit the ship, and no movement could be seen around. I assumed it was due to Citrine's children. My button down clung to me from the rain that fell over head, pushing my damp hair out of my eyes I looked to the others.

"Citrine's children took out the outside guards and any in the surrounding area." Arthur explained, "thank you for that Citrine." He gave her a slight bow.

"Of course. They were delicious." She smiled a sweet smile in response.

"Um... that's nice?" Arthur arched a brow unsure how to respond to her response.

Argon chuckled and kissed the top of her head, "it is an acquired taste."

"Clearly." Arthur locked his eyes on me. "Are you ready?"

I gave a nod to him, "I will follow you always into battle my Lord."

"Well, let us hope that this won't be a big battle and we can end this soon."
Arthur rested his hand on my shoulder, "we will split into two groups.
Chester, Argon, Sebastian, and Citrine you get as many of the innocent ones
and any held captive off the ship and through a portal to the inn. Agate and
Callen, you are with Merlin and me. Do you have the book you plan to use
Merlin?"
"Of course." With a flick of my wrist the leather-bound journal that was
outlined in amethyst with a clear quartz in the center.
"Good. Then let's go." Arthur gave the order and we separated from the
others.

The thick coat of dark energy felt suffocating. I held a small flame in
my hand to light the way through the thickness of the inky black energy.
"If it isn't my favorite wizard! Welcome to your end." Ophelia's voice
echoed around us. Picking up where her voice was coming from seemed to
cause problems. Tracking her energy back to her wasn't working. Her
energy was everywhere. It was just as before when I found myself in her
Purgatory only, she had turned the ship into that.
"Show yourself Ophelia." I said calmly to her.
Arthur kept his hand on the hilt of his sword letting his eyes try to search
the thick ink that coated around us. "Callen, Agate. Can you see her?" He
asked.
"She isn't on this floor. It seems she is channeling from another location."
Callen said keeping his eyes trained on our surrounding area. "Stairs head
up to the left."
"Come and find us Merlin. Careful to not get separated." Her voice held a
taste of malice while she spoke.
I clenched my jaw listening to her, her laughter echoing around us.
"Both of you keep your eyes peeled." I ordered as we walked forward and
eased down the stairs to the next floor.
It became increasingly colder on the next floor and the mixed energy was
unsettling. I knew who it was from, and it made me sick to my stomach.
"Watchout!" Agate sent a gust of wind past us making what was meant to
hit us shatter like glass. I assumed it was icicles. That was always Delemer's
favorite thing to toss at his enemies.
Laughter erupted from the ice demon as he clapped from wherever he was
located. "Bravo! It seems the little wind element still has it."
A low growl formed from Agate at the taunting coming from the demon,
"sorry I cannot say the same for you Delemer."

A slight scoff could be heard and the thick ink covering the demon melted away slightly into a low black fog. His eyes lingered over each of us until they landed back on me, and a smirk rested on his lips. "Well, well, well, how gracious of you to bring yourself to us wizard. It will make taking what we need that much easier. I don't necessarily need you conscious to get what I want out of you." A sick smile formed over his face at his words that made my skin crawl with his eyes that looked me over.

Arthur placed himself in Delemer's line of sight, "you won't be touching him. You will have to get your own smart-ass wizard. This one is taken."

I rolled my eyes and crossed my arms over my chest, "I am flattered but neither of you are my type."

"Smart-ass." Arthur glanced back at me with an amused smile on his face.

I chuckled in response, "so I have been told."

"You always did think you were better than us wizard. Always thought you were so smart. All the while you have always been nothing but peasant filth that won over a stupid princess's heart… well, I guess she wasn't just a princess, was she? Imagine my shock when I learned who she actually was. The angel Vretil. It is going to be wonderful having her. I can show her how a real man fucks." Delemer taunts.

I clenched my fists ready to rip him limb from limb, "Merlin." I looked at Stella who shook her head. "Ignore him. He wants to see you snap and you need to start doing the spell. Let the other three cover you so you can do this. They will only send their strongest after you because they want you. Remember this is your only chance you get at stopping them."

I unclenched my fist and let out a heavy sigh. I hated when someone else was right. *"You are right. Thank you."*

"What? No retaliation from the Great Merlin? I think you're losing your touch old man." His taunts continued. "Or are you getting tired of her? If that is the case it will be that much easier to take what I want."

"Okay, you're getting on my damn nerves." In one swift motion Callen had pulled back his bow and the arrows shot out hitting Delemer causing him to fall back.

An angry shout erupted from the ice demon as he jerked the arrows out of him. His white hair fell in front of his angry eyes, "damn elf!"

"I've been called worse." Callen already had his next set of arrows at the ready.

"Merlin, start the spell!" Arthur ordered and drew out his sword.

"Are you sure you can fight? You are still weak from what she did to you."

"Merlin, for once do as you are fucking told. I will be fine."

looked at his back with worry and pulled the book out. Allowing it to float, he pages flipped open to the page reserved for the ice demon. A light of gold came from the book, and I started the spell careful to not say it out loud. I locked eyes on Delemer and the clear anger from him was evident. He raised his hand and the area iced over helping him to melt into it.

"Where did he go?" Agate questioned.

"He is using the ice as a means to hide and attack us. Be on your guard." Callen kept his eyes focused searching every inch for any sign on the ice demon.

"Merlin, is the spell almost completed?" Arthur looked back at me, and I gave a nod.

"I just need him in the line of sight."

"Well, that doesn't seem to work right now." Agate looked around us.

"There!" Callen moved around jerking me out of the way as Arthur sliced the sword down taking off one of Delemer's arms.

Delemer let out a pained scream and retreated into the ice. "Now that wasn't very nice Arthur." A sick laugh left the ice demon from where he hid in the ice.

"That really was not nice Arthur and here I thought you played nice." A familiar flirty voice rang out.

"Keres." Arthur looked the girl over that held a childish pout over her lips.

"It wasn't nice of you to hurt my master. Now I must kill you. Oh, and hello Merlin. You look yummy."

I rolled my eyes and got back on my feet with the book still floating where it was waiting. "Hello Keres, still a psychotic child I see."

"Yes, this kitty still has her claws, and I am itching to sink them into you again."

"Should I be flattered?"

"Yes, I missed you. You make a fun scratching post." She flashed her sharp teeth at me and licked her lips.

"Careful Kitten. That book is what the old wizard plans to trap us in." Delemer's voice could be heard around us.

She pouted and looked me over, "still such a stick in the mud. I just got out of that silly crystal, and I do not plan to go back into anything. I want to play."

"Well, if you weren't the way you are then we would spare you but because you bring nothing but death and chaos then you will have to be sealed away. You and your brothers." Arthur explained getting her eyes averted back on him.

She bit her lower lip and looked him over curiously, "I am not sure which version of you is the most attractive. Your past you or this one. You have pretty hair that I want to play with."

Stella nods for me to look down and I quickly move Arthur out of the way and felt a sharp pain sink deep into my side before being jerked out. The book stopped floating and started to drop but Agate caught it and looked down at me where I had dropped to a knee holding my side.

"Merlin…" Arthur was quick to return to my side looking me over with worry. "Why would you do that?"

"Because I am an idiot I guess." I said with dry sarcasm and looked to meet his eyes, "you are my king and no matter what Arthur I took a vow to serve and protect you. Camelot may be gone but you are not. I will not let you die."

Arthur looked at me with a hurt look and went to help me up.

"Watch it!" Agate threw up his free hand and shielded us with a heavy gust of wind that sliced through what Keres threw at us. Coating the objects in the wind they exploded and the amplitude of it threw us back even with them being covered.

Covering Arthur with my body I winced at the heat that came off the explosion. He looked up at me shocked. "Stop trying to save me!"

"If I did that you would have been dead a long time ago before you came to rule over Camelot." I shifted off him and used the railing for support to ease myself up. Keres chaotic laughter echoed out as she jumped up and down clapping her hands like an excited child.

"That was so much fun! Let's do it again but with more of a big boom! I made some new toys. I hope you gentlemen enjoy them."

"Remember Kitten. We need Merlin in one piece." Delemer took his spot next to her and took her hand in his free one and kissed her fingers, "but I am very proud of what you did. I will make sure to give you a prize later for being such a good Kitten." His other arm that Arthur had cut off had been made into a blade. It was stained red at the end, and I knew it was used to try and kill Arthur but instead he stabbed me.

Chapter 12

"Merlin, you need to do the spell again." Callen said to me and took the book from Agate to hand to me. "Make it quick. We are wasting time with these two clowns."

Taking the book back I made it float again and the pages flipped back open. The gold light appeared, and I started back on the spell again repeating it in my head again. *'Cione Auferetur Quodperiit Malum Unus.'*

"Be a good girl and get that book for daddy Kitten." I scowled at Delemer's choice of words and kept at the spell.

"Yes daddy." Keres had a sickly-sweet smile on her face. Her movements mimicked that of a lioness ready to pounce on her prey. "Here little king it is time to play."

Gripping his sword in hand Arthur stepped away from me and stood his ground. "So, you fancy facing me on your own Keres. Are you sure that is wise?"

She giggled in response as she rocked back on her heels watching, "I fancy doing more with you than this but seeing as you want to put us away it doesn't seem I will get that chance. You must die young king. Quicker than that curse that is slowly killing you."

"Then let us make this quick. You two are in the way."

Callen looked down at me and I could see the rush in his eyes. "Are you okay? Are you sure this will work?"

"It has to." I replied as the book glowed brighter. "Arthur's life depends on it."

"But you're still bleeding out. Why are you not healing?"

"I would assume it has to do with us being in Ophelia's Purgatory. She is controlling the flow of energy and it is taking longer for me to heal and for this spell to take effect."

"Do you need to drink my blood?" Agate questioned.

I swallowed hard and moved my hand from the wound. Pulling up my shirt slightly I could see how bad it was. I wasn't stabbed by anything natural, and it wasn't just me bleeding out affecting me. The ice was laced with something. I gave Agate a nod. I was not a fan of drinking their blood but if it would heal me then I would.

Biting into his hand the wind element drew blood then pressed his palm to my lips. The iron taste coated my tongue and slid down my throat. Pulling his hand away he looked me over with worry.

"Did it help?"

I licked my lips and let out a shaky breath and winced at the pain. I shook my head and gripped the railing. "At least not yet."

I watched Arthur grip the hilt of Excalibur between both of his hands. His eyes never leaving the villainess. Her steps were graceful as she moved. It was almost like a ballet the way she moved. She moved in swiftly not missing a step, but Arthur seemed to be just as quick as her to move out of her line of fire. He swung his sword to strike her, and she ducked gracefully out of the way.

Delemer kept his eyes locked on me. A sick and twisted smile formed over his face, "feeling under the weather Merlin? You don't look so good. Feeling drained? It seems you are struggling to keep your little spell going and healing yourself." He taunted.

I gritted my teeth together as sweat ran down my brow. I focused on the book pushing away the pain and fatigue I was feeling from the wound on my side. My vision wanted to blur over, and I knew if I did that it was game over for all of us.

"Struggle all you like little wizard, but this is a battle you will not win. This is your end."

Arthur looked back at me with worry which only caused him to be caught off guard by Keres when she struck him.

"Arthur, pay attention. I am fine."

"The hell you are. You look worse than how I feel."

"Shut it Arthur, we can compare wounds later."

"Stubborn old man."

"You're one to talk."

"This lovers' quarrel is cute and all but can you both get back to what is going on?" Agate interjected.

Arthur and I looked at one another one more time. He gave a cocky smirk like he used to and quickly blocked Keres next attack.

She looked between us, "are you two a couple now?"

"What? No! He is a pompous pain in the ass." Arthur argued with a slight blush on his cheeks.

"Ah you are blushing! You are still in love with the wizard like before." Keres jumped back a little and clapped her hands excitedly. "That is so cute."

"Oh, good lord." Arthur rolled his eyes and took a step back catching his breath while the female was distracted.

"Keres dear, you are getting distracted. Stop playing and kill him." Delemer looked down at his nails while he tapped his foot in annoyance.
"Oh, yes. Sorry Master." A small pout rested on her lips, but she stopped and took a few steps back. "We need to go. The book…" She looked back at him with big, scared eyes.
Delemer was quick to move to jerk her out of the way as the pull drew him into the book. Keres screamed out a heart-breaking cry from across the room.
"Delemer!"
I looked down to see the image of his sharp feature in the book with his description on the next page. "One down. More to go." I said through struggled shaky breathing.
"No! Damn you, Merlin! Damn you!" She got to her feet as angry tears rolled down her porcelain cheeks. "I will kill you!" Rage radiated off her Her movements were fast. It was hard to keep up with her given the state that I was in. I felt like I was barely above water, and I was slowly drowning. I had hoped that sealing the ice demon away would take what he had done away, but it didn't. Throwing up my hand I placed a shield around my friends and I. With force from her I watched it crack.
"Give him back!" She beat down on the shield screaming in anger. "Give him back!"
"Trust me, you will be joining him soon." I replied coldly.
"Merlin, you are using up too much energy." Agate took over creating a shield and I collapsed to my knees working to catch my breath and keep my eyes open.
"We need to get you out of here so you can heal properly. We cannot go on with you in this state." Callen pulled my arm over his shoulder to support me. "You have lost too much blood."
I wanted to argue against it, but I knew he was right, and I was too weak to even object.
In a rush of wind Agate made us vanish. It was always an amusing trick of his. Landing on the steps outside the inn, Arthur got the door open and Callen quickly got me in.

"Elijah…" MaryBell's voice went shaky and her eyes wide at the sight of me. She yelled for help, "Judson!" I heard her shout as I started to not be able to stay awake.

Judson rushed around the corner, and I saw him with blurred vision. "Oh, Jesus Christ what happened? We need to get him on a bed."

"I can carry him. Just show me where his room is." Callen said to them calmly.

"Where is Clara?" I managed out weakly.

"She is tending to some that are hurt." MaryBell said gently, "do you want me to…"

"Merlin…"

My heart stopped at the sound of her voice and how scared and hurt it was.

"Princess… I told you I would be back." I teased weakly before falling into a state of unconsciousness and the last thing I heard was Clara's franticly calling my name mixed with some of the other voices around.

Chapter 13

'This will be your resting place, Merlin. Make good of the time you have because you do not have long before we finally get our hands on you and on her.'

I shot up in the bed with sweat running down my face, startled from the voice I had heard in my time passed out. Panting I felt my side that was still sore from where I had been stabbed. I looked down at it to see it bandaged up and saw Clara asleep next to me in a chair with her head rested on the bed. I smiled a tired smile and reached to take her hand and ran my thumb over her knuckles.

"Clara." I whispered to her softly. The voice still rang in my ears that I had heard in my time unconscious.

She shifted in her seat and let out a slow groan. Her eyes fluttered open, and she quickly sat up when she realized I was awake. Pushing up out of her seat she flung her arms around my neck. I laughed softly at her actions and winced at the slight pain from my side. "Easy my dear. I am here. I am alright. Have you been with me this whole time?"

"Of course, I was so scared. You have been out for days Merlin. I am sorry… did I hurt you?" Clara pulled away from me slightly and looked me over with worry. Taking one of her hands her fingers gently traced the bandage that was over my wound. Her eyes started to water up from the sight of it.

I took her hand that she had been tracing over the wound and kissed her fingers gently. "I am fine my dear Clara. Please do not cry. I am sorry I scared you."

"I thought… I thought I was going to lose you. You weren't healing and you always heal… I couldn't understand what had happened."

"I once again underestimated her. I keep thinking we get the upper hand but… I continue to be wrong. I did not account for this. I knew she could make our powers limited but I did not expect that. I have Delemer sealed away in the book. I was trying to work on Keres next. She has gotten even more revolting to deal with." I rubbed my eyes and let out a heavy sigh that sent a sharp pain down to my side. "Shit."

"Do you need me to get you anything? Why did you not call on Amethyst to help you?"

"I did not want him getting hurt. I was worried for what could have happened to him with the trouble I was already having."

She was silent for a moment and gave a nod. "I see. Well. You ignored my other question."

"Right. My apologies. No, I am going to be just fine. Let me just get up and dressed. We can have tea. Have you been eating?" I shifted to get up the slight pain stabbing into me that I worked to push away.

"You should be resting. You should not be getting up and moving around so much." Pressing her hands on my chest to try and get me to lay back down I pulled her in to me and tilted her chin up kissing her lips deeply. Pulling away slightly her blood rushed to her cheeks tinting them over.

"Clara, I am fine. You do not have to worry for me. I will be just fine. I have much to discuss with the others. We need to plan for a better course of action." I shifted off the bed and ease up. She looked me over with worry that I returned with a gentle smile. "Please do not worry my dear. I promise all will be well."

Grabbing up a fresh change of clothes I slipped into the bathroom to get cleaned up. I rested my hands on the cool marble counter and closed my eyes letting out a shaky breath. Looking back at the place I had been stabbed I straightened up and pulled the bandage back to see the spot. It looked better than it had but it was black around the area and veined out and was still hot to the touch.

"That does not look good Daniel. What is it?" I looked up to see Stella watching me with the same worried look as Clara had when I was in the bedroom.

'A side effect from the poison. A curse. I am going to work on undoing it the best that I can, but I just cannot let them know. I have the pain under control for the most part. I am going to have to get it completely under control before we deal with Ophelia again. If not, I fear what might happen.'

Her green optics looked the place over before moving up to meet my eyes, "you're dying... aren't you?"

I avoided her eyes and turned on the water to the shower. *'You should go. I need to shower.'* I avoided her question. I was not even sure myself if I was or not and I did not want to face it if I was.

"Daniel, you cannot avoid the topic. If you are you have to tell them."

I look back at her with an annoyed tired look. She shook her head and let out a heavy sigh of her own before vanishing for the time being.

In the shower I leaned back on the cool stone wall and let the water run down me. It stung my skin and the place I was stabbed. I swallowed back pained tears and closed my eyes working to calm my mind. Once again, she bested me. It was as if she knew my moves on the chessboard before I did. Hitting the shower wall with the back of my fist I gritted my teeth together with anger that had built up in me. Turning the water off I got out and dried off. I went through the motions of getting ready and covering the wound back up. I looked back at my reflection, and I could see it in my eyes how drained I was and how much what had happened had taken a toll on me. Shaking my head, I composed myself to fake off that everything was fine and normal. That I wasn't in fact dying. And like hell was I going to.

Walking down the stairs and into the dining room the group paused when they saw me enter. Relief seemed to wash over them that I was finally up. Lilith was up out of her chair running to me. Wrapping her arms around me hugging me she looked up at me with worried eyes and tears rolling down her face. I lifted her up into my arms and cleaned her tears away. "Now what is all of this? Why are you crying little one?" I asked her in a soft voice. She wrapped her arms around my neck and cried into it. I waited a moment before joining the others giving her time to let out all her worries. I could see some of them fighting back tears of their own over the little moment with Lilith.

"You're alive. I was so scared. Sissy was scared also. You weren't waking up and no one knew what to do. Not even the immortals. But you are awake and and…"

"Shh calm down Lilith. I am quite alright. Please do not cry over me."

"And why not? We all love you and would be sad if we lost you."

I opened my mouth but closed it. I did not know how to respond to her.

"Lilith dear let's let him sit down. He still should not be doing too much and really should not be carrying you." Clara said to her gently and nods for me to take a seat and Sebastian took back Lilith.

"You know I do not need to be coddled. I am just fine, and she weighs absolutely nothing."

"I do not care. We do not need the wound opening back up again."

I sigh heavily and rubbed my eyes. "Fine. Okay, did you manage to get everyone out that needed saving Argon?"

98

"Yes, we did. The Knights were gracious enough to offer them solitude here until we get things resolved and ended with what is going on. They offered them free stay and meals for them working. They are definitely not understaffed." The earth elemental leaned back in his chair at the long table with his arms crossed over his chest.

Rubbing my chin in thought a nod to his remark. "Good. That is less we have to worry on for anyone being in the way." Looking up I see the elderly couple coming out to see me. They both held the same worried look as the others.

"Now you are not supposed to be up." MaryBelle scolded me when she got to the table.

"So, I have been told."

"Don't give me lip. I want you in bed recovering."

"I-"

She gave me a crossed look that I returned with a scowl.

Jud chuckled at the interaction between us and sat down the cup of tea in front of me with milk on the side. "Now now MaryBelle. He don't heal like we do. I would say he is good to go now. Aren't cha son?" He slaps my back then pats my shoulder.

I hold back the hint of pain from being shown by the playful slap. "Yes, I am quite well. Only sore is all." I nod to Jud, "thank you for the tea."

"Of course. I will get you some grub. Also, there is a little baby I think that will love to see you. I will bring him out here." He nods for MaryBelle to follow him back into the kitchen.

She let out a sigh and rubbed the top of my head before kissing it, "I am just glad you are alive. You had us all scared to death. Don't do that again."

I watched her walk away and vanish into the kitchen. I looked back into my teacup and started to fix it. My side throbbed painfully but I held in the need to react to it.

"Okay, so we have Delemer sealed away. That leaves his sister, Mortem, Areses, Ophelia, and the Seven Sages. It is still a long list, but it can be done. We need a way to bring them out of Ophelia's little Purgatory. They have the advantage in there. We have to even the playing field and get them where we can handle them and not be limited like we were." I paused to take a sip of my tea and glanced at the others over my teacup. "I am open to suggestions."

"We would need to get them out here and with those objects they plan to use on you." Jenna tapped the side of her teacup in thought.

"We need someone to be the bait." Chester chimes in with a mouth full of food.

"That is easy enough I-"

"I'll do it." I snapped my head around to look at Clara with a shocked expression.

"Like hell I am letting you do that!" I raised my voice slightly, but she only looked at me.

"I was not asking you for permission."

"Clara, Merlin is right. We cannot let you do that. What if something goes wrong? You have Noah to think of." Sebastian argued.

"Then I guess you all should work quickly then to make sure nothing does." Clara expression was unmoved as she sat sipping her tea. "Now then, I am the bait. Where are we doing this at?"

"Have you lost your damn mind Clara?" I put my cup down and glared at her. I could feel my anger building up in me.

"According to my track record I lost my mind a long time ago in my past lives when I fell in love with you and never stopped. Look, you are not the only one that can handle themselves. I am not as helpless as you want to think that I am because you know that I am skilled, and I can protect myself. I am doing this. It will pull attention from you long enough for you to do what needs to be to get it done."

I ran my fingers through my shaggy dark hair and licked my lips working to calm myself down.

"Let her do it." Jenna chimes in.

"We will be hidden and can assist her. Are any of the lamps in the park lit with gas?" Carnelian spoke up and questioned when Jud came back out with Noah that was over the moon to see me.

Jud placed Noah in my arms that jumped up and down in excitement. "Yes. I believe some of them still ran on gas. Why?"

"I can use that to hide and watch. If it is near water Citrine can cover in the waters. Argon and Callen can use the nature to their advantage. Agate of course can take to the sky." She laid out the plan for them that I had to admit sounded promising.

'You are still hurt.' Noah's voice clicked in my head, and I looked down at him calming down and his little hand rested on my side.

'Yes, but I will be fine.'

'You are lying. I can feel it killing you.'

I was silent and didn't respond. I felt a warmth move over the spot and it started to glow a soft light blue. I looked down at him surprised. The others stopped talking as well and watched with wide eyes at Noah.

'Noah?'

'I am healing you.'

100

'But how?'

'I am your child.'

Pulling away his little hand he popped his thumb in his mouth and looked up at me smiling, "daddy!"

I blinked a few times trying to comprehend what just happened. I shifted him slightly and pulled up my button down and pulled back the bandage slightly and saw that it was gone. Any trace of it was completely gone.

'You are full of surprises just like your mum.'

He smiled up at me still sucking on his thumb. I pulled my shirt down and looked back at the others that still had a shocked look.

"Did he?" Chester looked at the baby with wide eyes.

"Um, yes." I replied with a slight chuckle.

"So, you weren't well, and you lied." Clara jabbed.

I sighed and gave her a side glance that was met with eyes filled with betrayal.

"Clara, do not give me that look." I looked back at Noah and arch my brow. "Can you do what you did for me for Arthur?"

Noah tilted his head at my word with his thumb still in his mouth. *'Maybe. Give me to him.'*

'I still cannot get over I am having a conversation with a baby. You are clever.' I get up and go over to Arthur. Arthur looks up at me with an arched brow and look of question. "Just give him a chance. I think he gained a bit of Clara's divinity and has a unique gift for healing. He can also talk… long story. Point is he is a gifted child, and he knows it. He has a better understanding of things than any of you are aware of."

Arthur takes Noah into his arms and watched the small child closely. Noah took his small hands and pressed them to Arthur's chest. We all watched the same soft blue glow form and cover Arthur's chest. He looked up at me shocked and then back at the baby.

"How is this possible?" Sebastian questioned from where he was sat with Lilith on his lap that was also watching in wonder.

"We have ourselves a powerful little mage. He will give you a run for your money Merlin." Argon teased and offered a small clap to the little baby when he lowered his hand from Arthur's chest and held up his arms from me to take him again.

I laughed softly in response to Argon's teasing and picked Noah up and kissed the top of his curly blonde locks, "yes, it seems so."

Chapter 14

Sitting back down at the table Jud took Noah back to the kitchen with him to take him outside to let him play on a blanket. At least that is what he said. More than likely, he would rope Noah in to snagging some sweeties. Jud did always have a sweet tooth and after all these years that hasn't changed. Sipping on my tea I sat in thought on what Noah had just done as the others chatted over what to plan to seal the others away in the book. I knew if they realized just what the child could do his life would be in danger. He was indeed powerful and would grow to surpass me due to gaining his mother's powers from a past life and from gaining mine. It was clear he was a clever child and would not show all he could do. He had not been thus far. He is like a grown person in the body of a small baby. "Merlin."

Hearing my name, I was pulled out of my thoughts and looked up to see the others watching me. "Sorry. I was lost in my own thoughts."

"What could be on your mind to miss the plan? That isn't like you." Heather says gently to me.

I licked my lips and ran my fingers through my hair, "Noah is powerful and if they learn of that they will come for him, and he will be a large target." Silence sat in. Clara paled at my words.

"We won't let them find out. This all stays between us here." Sebastian says.

"Like hell anyone is taking my kid." Clara's voice was cold and icy.

"Let's move on from this topic. Clara is going to arrange to meet with Wesley at the park to talk things through. Well, act like it." Argon chimes in tapping his fingers on the desk.

"Wesley? You are actually going to meet with him?" I clinch my jaw at the thought. "What if he hurts you?"

"He won't hurt me. He does love me. We talk and we are both out in the open. From there the others can set up and be ready for when they do come out."

I sat silently glaring down into the teacup that was squeezed between my hands.

Clara rested her hand on my shoulder, but I did not look up at her, "Merlin... Merlin this is the best option for now. I know you are worried.

We all are but we are running out of time and options. We must give this a go. At least have a chance to seal more of them away and then come up with a better plan. We cannot exactly Scooby-Doo this and use a trap from Freddy."

"Did you just make a joke?" I looked at her in a confused but slightly amused manner.

"Maybe."

"It was horrible."

"I know."

Her voice was soft as she spoke to me and rested her chin on my shoulder and stroked my cheek.

Glancing up to the chuckling coming from Chester I rolled my eyes.

"You both are funny." Chester stuffed a pastry in his mouth making some of the filling drip out onto his chin.

"You have a bit of something on you." I point out.

He looks down cross eyed and tried to lick it up with his tongue. He always reminded me of an overgrown child when it came to eating. Heather took her napkin and cleaned up the mess he had made on his face and then kissed his lips sweetly. He looked down at her with a look of adoration before pulling her in to kiss her lips a bit more deeply and tenderly.

Sebastian moved to cover Lilith's eyes with his hand, only for her to move it down a bit and gave a sweet mischievous smile. "I call dibs on flower girl when you both get married."

Heather blushed a soft shade of pink and hid her face in Chester's chest. "Of course, you will be, and Noah will be the keeper of the ring." Chester smiled a big smile and looked back down at Heather who peaked her head up to look at him.

Argon cleared his throat, "back on subject. We can come back to the wedding planning later. Chester must pop the question first. Anyways, Merlin, we must get you placed. You need to mask your energy so they cannot know you are there. Callen and I can keep you hidden out of sight so you can get the book ready."

"I guess we do not have any other way… okay, but if I see something go wrong, I am pulling Clara out of there."

"Do not worry. I can drop down from the sky and pull her out." Agate chimes in and gave a wink. "I can be your Super Man your majesty." I glared at him, and Clara only seemed to laugh at his pop culture reference.

"Lighten up Merlin. I am only teasing."

"Just mind your hands or I will gladly cut them off." I replied coldly.

"Anyways, when are we planning to do this? The longer we wait the more they have a chance to take in more innocents that would be caught in the crossfire of things."

"Clara first needs to contact Wesley first." Argon replies.

"I will call after breakfast."

"Good. If he agrees, which he will, then we can expect to try hopefully by tomorrow."

Silence overwhelmed the table once again allowing me to get lost in my thoughts. I had to stay one step ahead on Ophelia. So far that had not been the case and it was costing me a great deal. I had to think of something. I knew this plan was not going to be enough to stop her, I just didn't know what.

"Yes, the park. Meet by the water?" Clara was on the phone with Wesley arranging to meet up with him. I still hated the idea but there was no other choice. "Tomorrow. Yes... 6:00." She was silent for a moment. I could see how sad she looked, and guilt seemed to wash over her. I tried to avoid listening in on the conversation, but he made it difficult. "I will see you then. Yeah... love you too." She said in a sad whisper. I scowled at her last words to him before she looked at me after she ended the call. "Wesley will meet me. Which I guess you all heard that."

"We did. You did good Clara. Now we will all rest up for tomorrow. We will need it." Arthur said to us, "I also got to thinking. We should secure the area for the trap, so they do not have anywhere to run. They will be stuck within the perimeter."

"That is a good idea. We will be noticed if we set it. Citrine. Can you get something to your daughters for me?" I looked back at Citrine that gave a quick nod in response. With a wave of my hand a purple velvet bag appeared in my other hand. "Take these. They are Clear Quartz. There is four of them. Have them placed around the perimeter to where Clara will be meeting Wesley. Once it is set and we are there tomorrow Sebastian can set the spell to be locked in place. They won't be able to get out if it is done right. As for any of us we will be able to move in and out freely. That will help with getting Clara out of the line of fire."

"We have to keep Wesley safe also." Clara spoke up. I glanced down at her with slight annoyance at her words. I would have left him to die but that would only gain grief from Clara over it. "He is still innocent. He doesn't know what the council is or who any of them are. He just wants Noah and I back with him."

I sucked on the front of my teeth at her words and crossed my arms over my chest working to keep myself in check. "Fine. Save the royal prick if needed."

Pinching my arm, I scowl down at Clara who gave me a cross look. "Be nice."

"What is the spell you want me to use Merlin?" Sebastian interjected from where he sat in an armchair with a cigarette in between his fingers and a glass of brandy in the other.

Citrine looked the bag over that I had handed her then rested her eyes back on me. "I will get Analisia and Cicila on it. See you all soon." She took a step back and vanished into the shadows in the room.

Putting my attention back on Sebastian I took a seat behind Jud's desk and pulled out a sheet of parchment and a pen to write down the spell for him to go over. "Now you have to say it all just right and on point or it will not work." I got up and gave him the paper that had *captionem restring custodia* written on it.

Taking the paper from me he read it over and gave a nod. "Simple enough." He looked it over one more time before tucking it away in his inside suite jacket pocket.

"Everything is set in place. Let's give this another shot. We at least need to get some of them sealed away." Carnelian chimes in.

"Ophelia more than likely will not show herself. She will send the others to do her dirty work. That much we should account for. Keres will be ready to get her revenge. She will be unstable and that should make her an easier target to handle." Arthur added, "she made it pretty clear there is not anything she will not do to get her lover back."

"You are right on that. Be careful around her. Keres is a ticking time bomb. Delemer means everything to her, and she will do anything to get him back." I explained. "She is sick and twisted and will stop at nothing to ensure she gets him back. Ophelia more than likely has made Keres believe she can bring him back if it means she gets her hands on the book and on me. We cannot let that happen."

"That is where the ward will come in and you doing the spell to set it Sebastian. Even if she got her hands on the book or Merlin, she would not be able to escape anywhere, none of them could. Trapping them in what is set, leaving us being able to get in and out and them unable to do that."

"Exactly. We will and should be able to trap all of them. I cannot say that it won't be hard, it will be. We will work as quickly as we can. The book can only do them one at a time taking in every bit of them and documenting

them and their history." My eyes looked each of them over. The feeling of worry and desperation hung in the air of the study.

"You may all be excused. Take a break today. We won't have much of one tomorrow."

The breeze rustled the leaves and the sun hung low over the inn. I rolled the cigarette around in my fingers that I had bummed off Chester. It was not a habit I did much of unless I felt stressed, and I had reached that point again. Placing it between my lips I let it and took a long drag of it letting the heat of the nicotine burn my chest and throat. The trees were starting to go bare as the leaves covered the ground with their burnt colours of orange and red. I always enjoyed the smell and feeling of fall. The air was always crisp and calming. Unfortunately, it seemed that was not the case now. The energy in the air was almost electrifying. I took another hit from the cigarette working to keep my mind calm that was only running through every way something could go wrong.

"Lost in thought?" I heard a voice that made me grimace.

"Tiffany. What do you want?"

She walked over to me where I sat on the steps of the back porch. "I wanted to check on you. You seem under a lot of stress. Thought you could use a drink." She held up a bottle of scotch and two glasses before sitting next to me.

"You have to be joking. You expect me to drink with you and carry on like you aren't working for the woman that is trying to kill me and my friends and take my lover away?"

Giving a smirk she poured the two glasses and handed me one of them and took a sip of hers. "Yes, I do. I do have the hots for you after all and I am not giving up on making something happen. You can do better than her."

At this rate I was going to have to go buy a whole packet of cigarettes and I was not in the mood to do that, "Tiffany. Why on earth do you think I would give you the time of day to think I could be remotely interested in you in any way?" I took a swig of the scotch and looked back at her.

She got up and moved in front of me placing both hands on either side of me and leaned in to me with a seductive smirk on her lips, "because I always get what I want and I want you." Her lips locked on to mine and I found myself pulling away.

"What do you think you are doing?"

I looked around to see Clara glaring at Tiffany. "Clara…"

"Hush. I am talking to her. I suggest you get away from him. He is mine."
Tiffany leaned up and looked Clara over with a challenging look, "really?
Last I checked you are a married woman."
"Not for long. Now get away from him."
"Or what?"
Clara crossed the porch and slapped the girl. It was loud enough to echo and
left a red print on the girl's face. "Get away from him or so help me they
will not find your body come morning."
Tiffany took a few steps back and glared at Clara. "Is that so? Yet you're
the one walking to your end. You won't beat Ophelia. All you will be to her
is a shell she can pull from. You will be nothing... your majesty." She did a
sarcastic bow. "Also. He is a wonderful kisser. I wonder what else he is
good at." She looked back at me, "give me a call when you're bored of her.
I am sure I can teach you a thing or two." She picked up the bottle and her
glass before walking back in.
"Clara I-"
"Shut up."
I looked down into the glass of scotch and gave a nod to her. She sat down
next to me and rested her head on my shoulder.
"You're such a dummy."
I sigh heavily in response and took another swig of the drink. "You're mad
at me."
"No."
"Yes"
"No, I am not. Stop talking."
"I should have not taken the drink or talked to her. I know."
"I said to stop talking."
"See. You are mad."
"Of course, I am! She is trying to take you from me. You are mine!" She sat
back up and looked at me with a scowl that was adorable to me.
I chuckled at her reaction and took another swig before finishing it to sit the
glass aside and pull Clara into my lap. "She will never have me. I am and
forever will be. Yours." I kiss her lips tenderly and rest my forehead on
hers. "Also, that was a killer slap." I kissed her fingers and palm of the hand
she had used to strike Tiffany.
Blood rushed to her cheeks and tinted over a light pink as she chewed on
her lower lip.
"And you threatened to kill her."
Poking her two index fingers together looking away I watched her getting
embarrassed. "Yes... well. She made me mad."

"You are adorable. Come. Let's go get Noah and get ready for bed."

Chapter 15

'Merlin, come to me. It is only a matter of time before you fall victim to all of this. Rather than fight it why not join me. I know you thirst for power. Join me. You know you want to.
Merlin...
Merlin...
Time is ticking and you are running out. Tick tock, tick tock. You will lose so why not just join me. Join me, Merlin. I will be seeing you very soon my sweet prince.'

I sat up quickly in bed with sweat rolling down my brow. Her eyes burnt into my memory. I looked out the window to see it was still dark. Looking down Clara was asleep with Noah curled up in her arms. I slipped out from under the covers to go splash water on my face. I turned on the water and splashed the cold water on my face. Ophelia's voice echoed out in my mind and left me shaking. She should have not been able to enter my thoughts, but she had found a way. Twice. She was toying with me. I dried my face and looked back at my reflection and saw her behind me. I quickly looked back to see her looking me over and ran her hand over my chest.
"You won't win this Merlin. You don't need this." She leaned up and whispered in my ear before she vanished taking my necklace with her.
My heart was pounding in my chest and my hand went to touch my chest.
"No..." I gripped the counter and my head felt like it was spinning and then I collapsed.
Light broke through the white curtains making me squint. My head was throbbing from where I was laying in bed. Opening my eyes more I looked around to see I was back in bed and the weight of my necklace as still rested on my chest. I sat up confused and looked myself over. "Was it all a dream?" I whispered out loud to myself.
"Are you okay?" Clara asked from where she was leaning on the doorframe of the restroom in one of my button downs that was slightly oversized on her but looked nice to see on her.
"Just a strange dream. I am fine." I wasn't going to tell her that I felt like I had a hangover and felt horrible. That she did not need to know.

Clara walked over to me and sat on the bed with me and wrapped her arms around me. "Are you sure you are okay? You look like you did not get any sleep."

I wrapped my arms around her frame and kissed along her neck and collarbone. "Yes, I am just fine. You look much better in my shirt than I do."

She took in a slight sharp breath and arched her neck for me to enjoy it more. "Hmm, Merlin… we should not do anything right now. The baby."

"I would like to put one of those in you." I teased in her ear before pulling away slightly leaving her flustered.

"You are so bad." She chewed on her lower lip working to calm down. Her face flushed over.

I got up and started to get dressed, "is that so? I could bring you to the bathroom and enjoy you in every way in there if you need me to."

"Merlin!" She whispered loudly and let out an embarrassed laugh.

"Problem?" I teased and buttoned up my white button down before slipping on my navy slacks and pulling out and slipping on a grey vest.

She looked me over before finally getting back up and came over to me wrapping her arms around my neck and smiled up at me. "We come back here tonight safe, and you can definitely work on making a baby with me."

I arched a brow and laughed softly in response, "oh really now? Then I guess I have something to look forward to."

"I guess so." She teased and then leaned up to kiss me. "I love you."

"And I love you, my princess."

"So, you took on the Italian accent for your mum and dad during this life?"

"Random question, but yes. Why?"

"I was so used to hearing the Italian growing up from you that it confused me when you just stopped with it." She worked on getting herself ready as she talked to me.

"Well, I had to fit the part. I could not very well live in an Italian home and have an English accent. So, I changed it a bit. Now I do not have to hide or do that anymore. They both know who I am. Even if father is a royal ass."

"I am glad your mum was able to leave him." Clara whispered out, "anyways." She giggled. "You pull off Italian well."

"As am I." I fixed my navy tie and looked back at her watching her slip on a forest green sweater and navy skirt. "Thank you. I have had time to perfect it and practice. Also, you look beautiful."

"You don't look too bad yourself."

"I am glad you think so." I kissed her forehead. "Now, time to dress Noah.

Noah was sat up on the bed playing with Amethyst. His laughter filling up the room as he laughed at my dragon that was making smoke rings to entertain him. Clara lifted Noah up into her arms and playfully kissed him making him laugh more.

"Okay my little mage, it is time to get you ready." Clara said to him and laid him back down on the bed to work on changing his nappy and dress him in colors that matched her.

"Do you need any help?" I offered as I watched her.

"If you can, check his bag and make sure it is full on supplies for him for today."

She nods to his bag and I picked it up, shuffling through it I pulled out the stuffed dragon that favored Amethyst and showed it to him. "Look, you have a twin." I teased him and he gave me an insulted look. "You are right, you look better. My apologies."

Clara laughed at our exchange as she lifted Noah back into her arms. His thumb in his mouth. With his free hand reaching for his plushie.

"What is so funny?" I pass Noah his dragon and picked up the bag that she had overly packed. "He is good to go."

"Wesley wants to see him. I told him tomorrow I would meet with him to let him get him." Clara ran her fingers through the blonde curls on Noah's head. "He misses him." She sighs sadly.

I frown and look away, "do you wish for me to join you when you do what?"

"I would very much like that." She touched my cheek and turns me to face her. "We're going to talk about a divorce tonight. My father is working on the papers."

I looked at her shocked. "How? Papers were signed for an arranged marriage."

"Wesley is king now. He makes his own rules. He knows I am unhappy and that I want to be with you. He is tired of fighting over all of this and how it is affecting both of our healths. He does not want our fighting to hurt Noah. So, he has agreed to us splitting up. It is for the best."

I looked at her still in shock until I could not help but smile and quickly kissed her deeply. Noah patted my chest and I pull away slightly to look down at the little boy smiling up at me then I looked back at her flushed face. "We should get down to the others."

"Yes. You are right." Clara worked to compose herself.

Leaving our room, we walked down the hallway passing Tiffany that was showing a guest to their room. She ignored Clara and looked me over before stopping at the door that an elderly couple would be staying at.

Chattering from the couple on how adorable Noah was excited Noah when they stopped to talk to him and then looked to Clara and me.

"He looks just like his mama. So cute. How old is he?"

Clara gave them a warm smile and worked to ignore Tiffany being near, "he is 9 months." She offered a warm smile in return.

"Such a big boy! He is so alert. He has the same serious blue eyes that you do daddy." The elderly woman said to me.

"Oh?" I was taken back at her words.

"He definitely has such a serious look for a baby. It looks like yours you just had, right down to your eye colour."

I couldn't help but smile. I did not correct them. "Have a nice stay…"

"Oh, the baby isn't his. He belongs to another. She is here having an affair." Tiffany quips in and I shot her a look to stay out of it, but she only smiled.

"But here is your room and here are your room keys. Enjoy your stay." She turns on her heels and wonders off down the hallway.

Clara's face flushed over, and I took her hand pulling her away from the elderly couple that was left looking at one another confused.

"Why can she not just leave us alone?"

"Because she is annoyingly fixated on me." I stopped us on the last step before we went to the dining room. "Are you okay?"

"Embarrassed, but I am fine."

"I would not speak too soon. Come see what they are covering on the news this morning." Jenna came around the corner to grab us and we followed her into the kitchen.

Wesley and Clara's image came up followed by the following words of scandal in the royal family with images of her and I together.

Clara paled. "I- what?"

"Turn it off." I ordered. Jud was quick to turn it off before we watched more of it.

"I- I…"

"Clara. Breathe." Sebastian said to her calmly and took Noah from her so I could take her in my arms. "What I want to know is where did some of those pictures come from? She was under covers in a private room."

"Is anyone renting the room next to mine?" I questioned MaryBelle.

"No. It is empty."

"Get Tiffany in here." I ordered. "I need to have another word with her." My blood was boiling as anger washed over me.

MaryBelle and Jud looked between one another confused, "Tiffany? We let her go after what happened with Clara the first time."

112

I looked back at them quickly. "What?"

"We just saw her. She was taking an elderly couple to a room."

"Stay here." I pulled away from Clara and nodded for Jenna to come with me.

"She's here?" Jud called out after me. "MaryBelle call the cops." I looked back to see him following us.

"She was here last night also." I explained to both as I took the stairs two at a time back up to the second floor in search for Tiffany. I make my way down the hall back to my room.

"You think she is watching you from the other room?" Jenna questioned.

"She has to be. The images that were sent in no one should have seen. If I had known, we were being watched I would have never done anything with Clara. Not until things were resolved."

Jud pulled the master key out and unlocked the door to the room next to mine and went in it with Jenna following him. I went back into mine and I searched over the room looking for anything out of place.

"This girl is mad." I mumbled to myself.

The door closes behind me and I hear it lock. "I see you figured it out. You are so very clever."

I looked back at her with my lips pierced together. "I really wish you hadn't of involved Jud and MaryBelle. I will have to deal with them later though."

"Like hell I would let you do anything to them. The authorities are on their way. Just turn yourself in."

She broke the handle off the door and a light grey glow came from her hand as she sealed the door off.

"What?"

"I thought you were cleverer than this Merlin. Have you not figured it out yet?" She walked over to me and pulled my tie twisting it around her hand before forcing me back on the bed and straddled me.

"Get off of me." I said through gritted teeth. Jud started to bang on the door and shove into it. She leaned down and started to kiss along my neck until I shoved her away, "I said to get off of me."

She started to laugh and looked at her nails and then to me, "I see your wheels turning to figure this out."

"Ophelia."

"Such a clever man you are. It took you longer than I thought it would for you to figure it out." She was quick to pin me back down. "Now why not let us have some fun."

"Go to hell. Get out of the girl's body and face me yourself."

113

"Now why would I do that. You won't hurt this flesh bag because they are innocent. It makes it much easier to get my way with you."

I swallowed hard and took in a sharp breath at her hand on my belt buckle. A loud bang sounded, and the door flung back with Jenna and Jud on the other side with anger written all over their faces. "Jenna, Judson." I breathed out in relief. "Careful. It isn't Tiffany."

"Let me guess. Ophelia hijacked another body." Jenna glared at the girl that was on me.

Ophelia let out an annoyed sigh and looked back at Jenna and Jud. "You both messed things up."

"Get off of him."

"Or how about you get out. We were having a moment."

"A moment of you trying to take advantage of him."

Jenna rolled up her sleeves and looked Ophelia over. "I don't care if I hurt the body you are using. I am not as much of a gentleman as he is. Now you can move, or I will force you."

Ophelia glared at Jenna and moved away from me. "No matter. He will become mine. One way or another. Just you wait and see."

In a cloud of grey smog, she left Tiffany's body leaving behind an odor of decay. Jud was quick to catch the young girl that collapsed.

The three of us looked at each other and then at Tiffany.

"She had no clue she was being used as a puppet."

"Will she be, okay?"

"Is she even breathing?"

Jud checked to see if she was breathing, and he paled. "Oh Christ..."

I moved off the bed and knelt to her to check her. "She has been dead for a week." I looked back at Jud who held a look of guilt. "There is nothing you could have done to save her. It seems she was killed as soon as Ophelia took her body over. She sucked all the life out of her. I am sorry."

Jenna sat back shaking her head. "God dammit. How did none of us pick up on this? How did she mask herself to get past everything for a week now?"

"I do not know but she did." I looked at the young girl sadly and recounted the first time meeting her when I had arrived. She was full of life and held some much care and love in her. I should have noticed that something was off when her mood changed. "God I am such an idiot."

"That makes two of us." Jud chimes in and looked back down at Tiffany. "What do I tell her family? The cops are on their way. We have a dead body now."

"Jenna, deal with the authorities. I will deal with her body." I ordered. "It will be for the best that I deal with it." I took her in my arms from Jud. "As far as you know she got away." Waving my hand with a slight flick of the wrist the door fixed back with ease.

"Where are you taking her?" Jud questioned.

"It is best you do not know. The less you know the better." With that I vanished leaving them to handle things back at the inn.

I reappeared in a graveyard in Wilmington and entered an open tomb. Looking around at the tomb I had taken her body I found an empty slot in one of the walls for a grave and gently placed her in it. I looked at her sadly and leaned back on the cool stone wall. I closed my mind and cleared my thoughts until I felt something shift. My eyes opened and an arm grabbed me from around the neck and another grabbed at my arms. The skeletons of the dead reached out grabbing at me as I broke free and backed away. I blinked and they were gone. Nothing was there. The tomb was empty aside from myself and Tiffany's body.

"What's happening to me?" I dropped to my knees and held my head in my hands. I was confused. I did not understand what was happening, but I knew it was linked to Ophelia. I looked back at my hands and could see myself shaking. "I need to pull it together. I have work to do and I cannot lose my whit's now." I pulled myself together and took a deep breath composing myself before vanishing out of the tomb.

Back at the inn I did not repeat what happened in the tomb or tell them where I took the girl's body. The cops investigated the inn and found where she had been taking the pictures and bugged my room. All for Ophelia's sick amusement and to torment Clara.

"How is Clara?" I questioned Sebastian when he came to sit next to me on the porch steps and passed me a cigarette out of his case.

Lighting his cigarette and then passed me the lighter I lit mine as well then gave him the lighter back, "Upset, embarrassed. Definitely now dreading meeting with Wesley. This is a huge affair scandal. Father is working to get everything pulled down and covered up. He has ordered Clara to not talk to anyone outside of us while he handles the situation with my help." He ran his fingers through his hair and took a long drag from his cigarette. "As for you, you have definitely caught the interest of others."

I rolled my eyes taking a hit from the cigarette, "This is going to lead to problems with us trying to do what needs to be done tonight."

"Hopefully not but I have a feeling you are going to be right."

"Let's hope I am wrong."

We sat silently on the porch steps as the sky clouded over and a low rumble crept over as the rain started to fall, dampening the ground.

"Of course, it would rain." Sebastian said with a heavy sigh.

"It adds to the drama." I replied dryly.

"Clearly."

"There you two are." I glanced back to see Chester slip out the back door to join us and took out a cigarette of his own to light. "More rain."

"Should add to the problems for tonight."

"Well, a hurricane is working its way up." Chester added.

"Really?"

"Yep."

"You realize we're sitting on the porch talking about the weather like three old men."

"You're one to talk. You are old."

"Oh, shut it. At least I don't look it."

"No. That would be creepy because of Clara."

"Let's not bring my sister into this mix. She is dealing with enough as it is."

"I am just teasing." Chester leant on the railing and glanced down at us, "Do you think someone will die tonight?"

I looked up at him and back at the rain. "Probably."

"Bummer."

"Yeah."

We sat watching the rain as time ticked by until we got up and decided to go back in. Before stepping into the back door Clara shoved past Sebastian and Chester to push me back. I looked at her shocked but saw anger written all over her face.

"You're just going to avoid me after all of that?"

"Clara?"

"Well?"

"I-?" I looked to Chester and Sebastian and back at Clara confused. "That was not my intentions. My apologies…" I stepped back from her and looked down at her and the anger that coated her expression. "I upset you this much by not being with you?"

"Merlin you are such a dummy sometimes. How can you be the smartest man I know and still be such a dummy?" Her eyes watered over and she turned on her heels to run off leaving me confused on the porch looking between Chester and Sebastian.

"What just happened?"

"For someone who can read minds you would think you could use that more to your advantage to avoid problems like this." Sebastian teased and stepped through the door.

I sighed heavily and rubbed my eyes. "I really am an idiot. I need to go find her."

"She is probably with Heather and Jenna. Be careful. Jenna might end up stealing your girl." Chester had a mischievous smile over his face. "She is fun to invite into the bedroom for a little threesome fun."

"I did not need to know that Chester."

"Nor did I."

"I am just saying. If you are needing some extra spice..."

"Chester, as much as I appreciate the unwanted story and advice I am pretty sure evidence has shown I do not need help in that area of my life so thank you. I am going to go find Clara now. Also I do not like to share what is mine." I walked away from them hearing a firm slap from behind me.

"Ouch! Bash what was that for?"

"For being the biggest idiot, I know."

I laughed to myself and went in search of Clara leaving the two friends to argue.

"Looking for yer girl?" Jud came up to me from where I was leaning on the wall before going up the stairs.

"Yes. I messed up."

"Eh, it happens from time to time son. We're not perfect by no means."

"Well, I can read minds yet a fail to do that because it is rude."

Jud chuckled and nods for me to come and join him to sit down in the lounge. "Take a seat boy. Let an old timer give you some advice." I took a seat across from him in an armchair. "I have been married for 63 years and I can tell you it has not been all sunshine and daisies. MaryBelle has wanted to leave me sometimes flat out and one day she actually did. I couldn't blame her. Even though I was still married and been through the roughness we went through in Nam I was still an idiot kid when it came to marriage and being a father. She dropped me off at my parents, pushed me out of the car and told them I was their problem." He chuckled and I did too. The image of a small woman shoving someone his size out of a car was an amusing image to see. "Of course, we worked things out and I stopped being such a heavy drinker. Now here we are. The best advice I can give you son is just to apologize and show her that you mean it. From my understanding she thinks you are avoiding her after what has been all over the press that is runnin'. Have you?"

I looked down at my hands that I had folded together, "no… yes…" I rested my head in my hands, "I don't know."

He was silent for a moment before getting to his feet. "She was with that boy with the long white hair. He took her to sit outside on the front porch. I don't know if they are still there, but you can check."

I looked up at Jud and gave him a sad tired smile. "Thank you, Judson."

"You've never had a father figure in your life to give you advice have ya?"

"No, not really. I did once but he passed away when I was young back in Camelot. He was my mentor. He was the castles healer before I was. One of the plagues took him from me."

Jud gave a sad nod and remembered the old man from what I had shown him from the first night here.

I got to my feet and held out my hand for him to take but he pulled me in to hug instead. I was not used to something like that even though he had hugged me before. I patted his back and he pulled away from me.

"Go get yer girl before pretty boy steals her from ya." He teased.

I rolled my eyes and let out a heavy sigh. "He would." I chuckled dryly and left Jud in the lounge to go out to the front porch of the inn. The rain had stopped. I looked around but did not see them, but I heard chatter coming from around the side of the house where one of the barns was at for the venue. Working my way down the steps over to the voices. Coming to a halt, I crossed my arms over my chest and glared at Arthur that had his arms wrapped around Clara from behind sitting under one of the big maple trees on a blanket.

"Am I interrupting something?"

Arthur looked up at me and sighs heavily but doesn't let her go. "Kinda."

I suck on the front of my teeth and looked to Clara who avoided my eyes. "Clara, can we talk. In private please."

She gave a nod and shifted to get up taking my hand. "Thank you for talking to me." Her voice was soft as she spoke to Arthur.

I looked back at him with a slight look of anger, and he matched my look. Keeping my fingers laced with hers I led us away from him.

"What the hell was that, Clara?"

"We were only talking. He was making me feel better. Today has been horrible and you haven't been around at all. You vanished and left me alone!"

I clenched my jaw and out of habit ran my fingers through my hair, "so you thought it a good idea to seek comfort in the arms of another? You realize anyone could get pictures of that and it will add to the scandal. Just because you are getting divorced does not clear you from the public eye. Plus, he has

118

a thing for you. He always has. Do you not remember two years ago he even challenged for you in the hallway of our school's house?"

"Yes. I remember."

"It hasn't stopped Clara."

"I know."

I looked at her and shook my head. "Look, I am sorry I was not here to help you and look after you. I had to handle the situation with Tiffany, and I just needed to clear my head. I got to talking to your brother." She was avoiding my eyes and kept her distance from me. That hurt probably the most, "Clara I am sorry."

"It's fine Merlin." She said softly.

I reached out to pull her to me, but she pulled away from me. "Clara…" Pain coated my voice.

"More is going on with you and you are hiding it. I don't know what it is, but I know you are hiding something."

I dropped my hand and looked away from her and leant up against one of the trees.

"I need to go. It is almost time to go meet Wesley." She turned to leave but I reached out to take her hand and pulled her around to face me. I locked my lips on hers and kissed her deeply. Thunder rolled over head indicating more rain coming in from the hurricane. Droplets sprinkled down over us as we kissed. She wrapped her arms around my neck, and I pulled her frame against mine not letting up on keeping my lips locked on hers and our tongues slipping over one another's with the rain slowly coming down over us dampening our clothes and hair.

I pulled away slowly and rested my forehead on hers and looked down into her blue optics, "I love you and I am sorry for how much pain I put you through. If you choose one of them then I do not blame you. I have done nothing but bring you pain and suffering in each life because of vendettas against me but no matter what I will never stop loving you. I will take a step back, but I will never stop loving you."

I watched as her tears mixed with the rain falling over us. She didn't say anything. She only leaned up to kiss me deeply again pushing me up against the tree I had leant up against only moments ago. My fingers tangled in her damp locks as she pressed herself against me. Pulling away she rested her forehead on my chest and lightly hit it with her fist.

"You dummy." She sobs out.

I wrap my arms around her and hold her to me. "I know." I kissed the top of her head, "let's get you inside so you can get dried off."

Guiding us back into the house I took us to our room and grabbed her a towel and wrapped it around her. "Shall I run you a hot bath?"

"Yes please." She whispered. Her eyes puffy and red from crying. We didn't say anymore on what happened. I ran her a hot bath in the claw foot tub and helped her to get undressed and into the tub leaving her a fresh towel and change of clothes before I went to leave the bathroom. "Stay."

"Hmm?"

"Stay with me. I do not wish to be alone."

I paused at the door and closed it. "As you wish." I went and sat by the tub and pulled my knees slightly to my chest. We sat silently for a long while with the sound of the rain beating down on the inn and the slight sloshing on her bath water being the only sounds heard.

"Merlin."

"Yes?"

"I love you."

"I love you too."

"You're still a dummy."

"I know."

A small smile crept over her face when she locked eyes on me. "But you're mine and that will never change." She let the water out of the tub.

Chapter 16

With luck the rain had eased up some. We were all in position. My heart was racing as I kept my eyes locked on Clara. She stood out in the open with an umbrella to keep the drizzling rain off her. She looked beautiful. Her navy trench coat pulled tightly around her. Catching sight of curly blonde hair walking up to Clara, I knew it was Wesley. Wesley stopped in front of her. He held his hand for her, and she took it. They both held looks of sadness as they stood and chatted.

"Where are they?" Argon questioned.

"Give it time. This has to work." Callen whispered back.

"Can you feel anything Merlin?"

I focused on everything around us pinpointing any shift in the energy.

"They're coming. I am not feeling Keres with them, but I do feel Mortem and Areses."

"How many are with them?"

"Maybe two more. I am not sure."

"Could they be hiding and masking like we are?"

"It is possible."

"Well, that does not sound reassuring." Argon mumbled as he watched Clara and Wesley. "You know, I actually feel for him. He is doing what I never could… instead I let my own jealousy eat at me and turn me into something horrible. He is a bigger man than I ever was or could be. Giving up the only woman he has or ever will love to allow her to be with the man she loves. It is killing him. His heart is breaking. If he did not have a kingdom and child to care for, I do believe he would lay down and die."

"She never wanted to be married to him in the first place." I did feel slight guilt over it all. "Plus, he was dead set on bringing me in."

"Yes. 'Was' is the operative word. He wants to call that off for Clara's sake, but the counsel won't stop. He does not know who the counsel actually is." I glanced at Argon and saw guilt in his eyes. "I have to let Citrine go." Callen frowns. He didn't say anything, but I could see the pity in his eyes for his father.

"I see." I looked back at Clara and Wesley. I watched Wesley rub his arm looking down at his dress shoes. He looked sad and broken. Clara didn't look any better. Her eyes were puffy again. It was evident she was crying.

My heart broke for her. The energy shifted and it seemed like silence settled in.

'Clever Merlin, you think your silly little plan will save your friends? How sadly mistaken you are. You will fail like you always do so why not join me? I can get rid of those Sages that hunt for you. All you have to do is join me.'

Ophelia's voice echoed in my head, *'get out of my head!'* I dropped to my knees working on keeping my vision in focus.

"Merlin?" Argon was knelt beside me trying to pull me out of my thoughts. "Merlin what is going on?"

The pressure lifted from her, and I started to breathe heavily. I looked over at the immortal, panting with my head throbbing. Looking back, I saw darkened over figures enter the perimeter. Sebastian started the spell from where he was at with Citrine and her daughter's, and it was set. I watched as Wesley pulled Clara behind him demanding to know what was going on.

"Merlin if you are okay you need to start the spell. Now." Callen ordered. I gave a nod and worked on the spell. The book floated in front of me illuminating the soft gold glow.

"What is the meaning of this?" I heard Wesley demand. "What are you doing here with those two?"

"Wesley... Wesley you need to run. Now." Clara pleaded with him pulling at his blaze.

"I will not. You three answer to me." Wesley turned to one of the figures. "What are you doing with those two? You are fraternizing with the enemy!"

Dark laughter came from one of the cloaked men. He stood a good bit taller than Wesley and took a dangerous step closer to him. I watched as Wesley kept Clara firmly behind him out of the larger man's reach that was cloaked in black with his hood pulled firmly up over his head.

"Answer me dammit!"

Laughter rolled out of the one that stood uncomfortably to close to Wesley. I watched as Wesley gritted his teeth, but he stood his ground.

"Jamenson. I demand to know what you are doing."

"How brave of you to try and protect her your majesty. We only want her. Turn her over and you won't have to suffer." Jamenson replied darkly.

"Where is Agate? He should be getting them out of there." Argon whispered loudly

"I don't know. We need to get them out." Callen chimes in, "Merlin keep doing the spell. You cannot stop."

"I can't not do something. Clara is out there."

"Yes, but we need this book working and collecting those men. You are the only one strong enough to keep the spell going."

I let out a shaky breath and clenched my jaw. Looking back at Clara that clung to Wesley and him not moving from protecting her.

"Now now, why protect someone who has been whoring around on you with filth like Merlin?" Mortem finally chimes in. "We only need her to pull him out of his little hiding place and then we can let her go." I knew he was lying. It was evident.

"Like hell I am letting her be left to the lot of you." Wesley said coldly. Areses must have finally had enough of the back-and-forth dance that was going on. He struck Wesley knocking him to the ground slicing into his chest and stomach.

"Wesley!" Clara shouted and dropped down next to him trying to stop the bleeding, "no…"

"Now for you your majesty." Jamenson chuckled and took a dangerous step close to her.

Clara's eyes darkened over from where she was on her knees covering Wesley. His blood running out mixing in with the rain washing it away. "Stay away." Her voice was icy.

They only chuckled. Jamenson reached for her, and she slapped his hand away then knocked him back with a powerful blast of her own white light. "I said stay away!" She slowly got to her feet and her whole demeanor changed. She was coated in energy I had not felt from her in a long time.

"The princess has claws I see."

"You're damn right I do."

"Oh boys." I heard Carnelian called out in a sing song voice from where she had perched herself on the railing near the water. She gave a little flirty wave and I watched Mortem melt slightly at the sight of her. "Awe Mortem. Want to still try to play with me? Come and get me then."

Mortem went to go to Carnelian, but Areses pulled him back.

"Think before you react. She is leading you into a trap." His father said to him.

Mortem looked Carnelian over from her dark tan legs up to her dark eyes taking in all her curves making him lick his lips in response with craving her. She gave him a wink and a seductive look. "What? Is daddy not going to come let you play little fire demon? We could really make some fire

123

together. Spark a flame with feeling you rubbing on me." She ran her fingers slowly over her body and inched her skirt up more. I had to admit. She was fantastic at acting and playing on Mortem's lust because he had always fancied her. "Come get me Mortem." She parted her legs, and he shook his father off.

"You are a fool Mortem." Areses said coldly.

Mortem smirked and looked back at him, "then I guess at least I might go down a happy man in the pleasure of her company."

Carnelian pulled the male to her placing him between her legs running her hands up his chest. Searching his pale face over. She bit her lower lip and pulled at his shirt for him to lower his neck and she kissed him. Wrapping her arms around his neck.

Argon and I looked at each other confused.

"What is she doing?" Callen questioned.

"I-?"

Before I could say more, she vanished with Mortem. Taking him into the flames of the lamps that were burning.

"What just happened?" Argon demanded.

Realization suddenly hit me. "She was spying for him." I said sadly. "She has been the inside man for Mortem." I let out a sad chuckle. "That is how Ophelia has been able to be one up on us this whole time.

Argon looked down at me with a look of betrayal coated all over it. Agate landed on the other side of Areses. He held the same hurt look as Argon. "I-I see…" Argon let out a hurt chuckle and shook his lower lip. "How is the spell, Merlin?"

"It is ready I just need to be in the line of fire for it to lock on and pull one of them in."

"Perfect." He nods to Agate that was dealing with Areses.

"I am going to go help Clara." Callen said to us.

"Be safe Callen."

"Always father." Callen gave his father a bow and was quick to move from us using the trees as cover, his bow drawn back and arrow at the ready.

"Ready to move Merlin?"

"Of course, your majesty."

"Then stay close. I will keep the illusion cloaking us, but I need you to work as quickly as you can."

Clara looked around herself and glanced over to see her brother slam his fist up against the side of one of the men's faces that had surrounded her. "Bash."

"Get away from my sister." He stood over the man glaring down at him. "Clara." He glanced up at her before moving quickly out of the way from the man that aimed to kill him.

"Be careful Sebastian." Clara said to him. She had placed herself to protect Wesley that was struggling to stay alive. "Wesley, stay with me. You cannot die."

Wesley laughed weakly and forced himself up using the metal bench for support. "Do not worry my dear. I am not going down easily."

Citrine appeared next to him and bit into her hand. "Drink. My blood will heal you."

I could tell he was not a fan of the idea, but he also did not like the fact Clara was fighting to keep him safe. Reluctantly he took Citrine's palm and drank her blood that was pooling up in it.

"How cute all of you think you can win. One of your own even turned on you. She played you all for fools. Even the great Merlin." Areses taunted. "It seems Carnelian found someone else to get under didn't she Agate. I guess you couldn't satisfy her the way she wanted."

Agate clenched his fists together and moved out of the way of Areses blow. It was easy to see he was trying to ignore Areses taunting but his words were cutting deeper than the blows he was attempting to land on the immortal.

"What? Has the taste of fire got your tongue?" Areses taunted more. Agate stumbled back and landed hard. The ground started to wrap around him pinning him to the damp earth as the rain continued to soak us. "How beautiful this moment is. Watching you struggle is ever so delicious. You would make a wonderful plaything for me." He knelt down to stroke Agate's cheek that made him flinch away.

"Go fuck yourself." Agate growled out and spat in the old king's face. In return the king slapped him. I flinched at the memories that flashed quickly in my mind from when he had me captive and the time spent at his mercy. I swallowed hard and blinked rapidly pushing the memories back. "Merlin, can you narrow in on Areses?"

Argon's voice broke my thoughts. I looked up at him and then to the old king that had a firm grip on Agate. "Yes, but I would risk pulling Agate in as well. He is too close to him."

"Dammit… okay, I can get him free. As soon as he is pulled back close in on Areses."

"Yes sir." I hated being in the position I was in. I wanted so desperately to be fighting and to protect them all. Handling the book was keeping me from that but it was our only option.

Argon worked quickly to try and pull Agate free of his bindings from where he was next to me, but Areses was not letting the elemental go that easy.

"Argon. Come out to play. I know it is you trying to manipulate what I have done so why not come out and fight for him face to face. You two always did have a special friendship, didn't you? Secret lovers maybe?"

Argon gritted his teeth together.

"You cannot go out there."

"He isn't taking him from me. Agate is mine."

I looked at him slightly puzzled until it hit me, "oh... Oh! You both... when?"

"On and off for quite a while."

"I see. So... does Citrine know?"

"She joins us."

"Uh... I really don't know how to respond to this so go get your boyfriend." To say I was shocked and confused was an understatement. The lack of me reading everyone's thoughts out of respect continued to only shock me when I learnt what went on behind closed doors.

Argon pats my shoulder and moves out from where he was hiding with me. "You have me. Now let him go." Argon ordered.

Areses chuckled and turned around to look at Argon with Agate trapped in his arms, "Look, your king and lover came to your rescue. How romantic." He teased. "So, are you really upset that your ex turned on you?"

"Let me go." Agate struggled against his bindings that only got tighter with every movement he made to try and break free. "Argon just do what has to be done to stop him. Don't worry about me."

"I am not losing you. Not again. I cannot go through that. Not again..."

"Argon..."

Argon swallowed hard and shook his head and looked back at Areses that held a sick smile across his face.

"Well, come get him Argon before I squeeze the life out of him."

'Come on Argon... hurry up. I just need one clean pathway and I can pull him in.' I said to myself.

'Merlin.'

Her voice echoed out in my thoughts sending a throbbing pain that made my skull feel as if it could burst open.

'No...' My eyes watered with the pressure of the pain making me want to lose focus.

'Merlin... don't fight it, Merlin. Come to me.'
'Never... get out of my head!'
'Not until you are mine.'
'I will never be yours.'
'We will see about that.'

The pressure let up and I dropped to my knees panting heavily blinking my vision back into focus.

"Sebastian!" I snapped my head up to watch something be pulled out of Sebastian and he collapsed to the ground with Clara catching him. I paled at the sight of the male unmoving on the ground with his blood pooling out around them.

"No...no!" The flash of red hair caught my eye at seeing Stella screaming out.

"Now then, that brother of yours is out of the way. Always in the way. Just like that father of yours." Jamenson said as he cleaned Sebastian's blood off the dagger he had in hand.

Citrine moved quickly in between them and motioned for her daughters to help Clara and Wesley move Sebastian's body out of the way.

"You three have to get out of here."

"No. We cannot leave you guys." Clara was rocking Sebastian in her arms. I could only faintly pick up on life from him. He was dying quickly.

"Clara, Sebastian is dying. Get him out of here. The girls can heal him, but you must go. Whatever happens do not come back here."

"Citrine..."

"Analisia. Cicilia. Get them out of here."

"Yes mama." The twins said in unison.

Clara looked around frantically until she locked eyes on where I was still covered. I watched her mouth *I love you* before they vanished out of sight with the girls.

"If it isn't the witch of the sea. Come to play?

"Come to kick your ass."

The man chuckled at her words but stopped when he watched her vanish into the puddles of water and jerked one of the men under screaming only to spout him out in my line of range. I took the cue and finished the spell that sucked the male in that Sebastian had punched into the book. Jamenson looked around himself at all the puddles of water and then where his mate had been and completely vanished.

"So, you are here Merlin. Too scared to come out and fight like a man?" He taunted.

I looked down at the book and read the name that came across for who had been sealed away and then looked back at Jamenson.

"Well Merlin? Are you going to keep letting women fight your battles?"

"Peek-a-boo." Citrine popped out from behind him and swiftly kicked him sending him to the ground. "You should be paying better attention." She stood over him with a smirk planted over her face.

"You little bitch." He said through gritted teeth and got back up on his feet.

"Oh yes daddy. Talk dirty to me." She teased and let a taunting smile spread over her.

Glancing at Argon I watched him muffle a laugh with focusing on Areses that was making it hard to get to him from him using Agate as a human shield.

I had almost forgotten about Callen when an arrow whizzed by striking the other male trying to grab at Citrine. She looked up to the trees to spot Callen carefully hidden and casting another arrow hitting Areses in the eye.

The old king screamed out and yanked at the arrow that had pierced into him taking his eye with him that stuck coated in blood onto the arrow. Losing his grip on Agate he fumbled back screaming in anger.

Citrine kicked the other male in my direction pressing the arrow into him more. "Bye bye now." She gave a little wave as he struggled to run from the pull of the book that trapped him away. "Now then Jamenson. You are next. I am pissed off and ready to take out all this on you, but I know Merlin is tired of holding the spell together to trap all your pathetic asses away so let's make this quick." Jamenson gritted his teeth and backed away from her. "Come on, come play with me. I am getting bored." She teased him. "I know. We can play a game of tag. Guess what. I am it. I will give you a head start to run."

Argon quickly pulled Agate into his arms. I never noticed that Agate had a smaller frame next to Argon that was almost feminine. Quickly looking Agate over from where I stood, I could see that thorns had sliced and punctured into the air element. He was leant in weakly into Argon, nuzzled into his chest using his lover for support. I furrowed my brow and looked him over again trying to feel his energy. I clenched my jaw at the realization that the thorns had poisoned him in the same manner as what had happened to me due to being stabbed by Delemer.

Disregarding being told to stay hidden I came out rushing over to them. "Argon you need to get him out of here…"

"Merlin you should have…"

"He is not well. He is suffering from the same thing that had been wrong with me when Delemer had stabbed me." I watched as Argon expression paled and he looked down at Agate that was quickly going faint.

"Agate… Agate stay with me…"

"Get him out of here." I ordered. Looking up moving to block Areses blow covering the two immortals with my own body. I gritted my teeth at the searing pain from the flames that lapped at my skin burning into my flesh. "Go. Now."

"Merlin!" Argon looked at me with shock. He moved back quickly with Agate cradled to him struggling to stay awake. "What about you three?"

"Argon, get out of here with him. We can handle this." Citrine interjected using the puddles from the on pouring rain to quench the fire that Areses had made. "Are you okay Merlin?"

Wincing at the wounds that were healing I looked down at my tattered chard button down and frowned slightly, "I really liked this shirt." Glancing back at the sea witch I gave her a nod, "I am fine, but someone owes me a new shirt after this."

She rolled her eyes and focused back on Jamenson that was looking to the trees trying to spot Callen and keep his focus on Citrine. He was losing at that. She vanished into the puddles again and pulled him under. A struggled scream as if he was drowning escaped him.

Argon hesitated to leave as he looked me over one last time. "Be safe. I will return as soon as I can. You get these last two sealed away and then we work on the rest… god speed."

I gave him a slight bow and watched him vanish. Feeling slight rumbling under my feet I stumbled back catching myself. Eyeing the book that was still hidden I looked around waiting for Citrine to spit Jamenson out so I could seal him away and focus on Areses that stood glaring at me with a look that always made my skin crawl.

"Now Merlin!" Callen called out as Citrine spit out a half drowned and drained Jamenson that struggled to crawl away from the puddle he had been released from.

I went to finish the spell and my heart dropped. The feeling of the vines started to wrap around me working up from my legs to my chest. Working to keep my mind focused on sealing away one of the Seven Sages and not letting past trauma triggers me felt more draining than the actual magick at work to keep the spell going.

Jamenson screamed and tried to claw and crawl away, but it was no use. He was added to the book.

All of a sudden I felt the pressure of a body against my back and the same sickly smell of death made me go pale.

The feel of him running his fingers along my neck and breath me in made my stomach turn, "it is so good to see you again Merlin. How I have missed the times I had with you. How about we revisit them again?" Areses said. "I would not do that if I were you. Let him go!" Citrine was quick. The heavy rain and water gave her a heavy advantage over the rest of her comrades, "let him go and you can keep your throat intact while you take your place in your new home. I would eat you but you're not my taste. I do not eat garbage."

I shuddered at her words and the feeling of his hands traveling over me while the vines tightened around me holding me in place.

"Darling Citrine. How amusing you are. If he finishes the spell, then he is taken with me and none of you can complete his work. So careful little mermaid. One wrong move and I will also pierce his heart with the same poison that I used on that adorable little air elemental. Your best option is to let me go and your hero here goes with me. Well, he is not really a hero. Are you mage? You are and always have been as much of a villain as I have been. Only our crimes for all the wrong we have done separate us on a thin line." His breath was hot against my neck as he pressed me more into him while he spoke into my ear.

Citrine looked up to Callen who kept his aim locked on Areses. I knew he was searching for a clean shot and weighing his options on what to do. He was a man of little words but used his silence to his advantage. "Now why not break these silly wards you had that pesky Cameron boy put up and get us out of here, hmm? I am Itching to sink myself into you again."

I held my breath and worked to not move too much. Each inch of movement to struggle only tightened his hold like a snake strangling its prey.

"That is not happening, and Merlin is a better man than you. You are not going to compare your crimes to his. He has done nothing as heinous as you have done." Citrine argued. "Now let him go."

"In the eyes of God my darling Citrine all sins are the same. Not one is worse than the others. If only you knew just how wrong you are about your dear precious Merlin."

"Do not preach to me of God. That one abandoned us all a long time ago." I could feel Citrine trying to hold it together and ignore his taunting and trashing of my honor. "I do not care what he has done in his past. Compared

to you he is a saint, and I will follow him until the end of time when this bloody planet is no more taking us with it."

His laugh was dark and made my skin crawl. It was becoming increasingly harder to breathe and stay conscious. I was running out of time and out of options on what to do. I finish the spell and he would take me with him into the book or I break the spell on the wards and he escapes taking me with him leaving Citrine and Callen behind to care for the book. If I went with him, he would have me where he wanted me again until Ophelia had her say and her having the dagger and chains to keep me bound.

"Merlin... you have to do something. You need to call on Amethyst. He can get you out of this." My blurred vision locked on Stella's worried eyes, "please call on him!"

With struggled breathing and what felt like could be my last breath before I would go limp, I called for out for him softly, "Amethyst. I need you old friend."

A rush of wind exploded around us with Amethyst roaring to life. I felt something sharp pierce into my chest, and I coughed out blood. Areses tossed me aside and I landed hard on the pavement.

"Merlin!" Citrine's voice sounded. Rushed footsteps ran over to me and I felt her pull me into her arms. She pressed her hand over my chest as she tried to stop the bleeding. "No... Merlin. You must stay awake. Why are you not healing? Come on..." She bit into her hand and pressed her palm to my lips. Tears and blood mixed with the rain that poured down around. I pulled her hand away from my lips and I shook my head and gave her a sad smile. "No. Don't you dare give up Merlin. Don't you dare fucking give up. You are going to seal this damn beast away and we will get you help. Just hang on."

I had a hard time keeping my eyes in focus to watch Amethyst, but I could hear him giving Areses a hard time. "Citrine... I cannot keep the spell going. I am sorry..." I whispered to her weakly. "Please forgive me."

"Merlin? Oh Neptune... Callen! Fall back! Grab the book!"

I blinked my eyes a few times struggling to not go under as my lungs filled with my own blood.

"Amethyst. Come on boy... We have to go..." Citrine's voice was rushed, and I felt her put more pressure on my chest.

"Why isn't he healing?"

"I don't know... this is worse than last time. I don't think he is going to make it."

Amethyst retreated into my ring, and I felt us starting to shift locations.

'Merlin... tick tock. Your life is running out. I can save you Merlin. You just have to join me.'
'I would rather die.'
'Now now, Merlin. Do not be so rash. Join me. We can rule together and bring everyone to their knees. All the power and everyone worshiping us like the gods we are.'
'Get out of my head... I will never join you or be yours.'
Ophelia's voice faded out with her mocking laughter.

"You can runaway for now, but this won't be the last you see and hear from us." Areses voice taunted, "see you soon Merlin. That is if you do not die before then. It will be such a shame to see you go before I have had my fun with you like I did before."
"You sick creep." Citrine's voice was shaky as she spoke.
"We're going." I heard Callen say.

My vision was gone and the weight of everything started to pull me under more and more giving the feeling of drowning and I was, in my own blood. "We're losing him." Citrine said as I felt us enter back into the inn. She screamed for help and footsteps rushed to us.

"No... Merlin!" Clara's voice sounded and I felt her hands on me pulling her in to hold me to her, "no... no Merlin. Don't leave me. Merlin... You promised..." She sobbed into my neck pleading with me to not leave her. That was the last voice I heard as I got pulled under. Darkness unfolded and that was all I saw. It was only fitting. I would never see the gates of gold that everyone goes on about. God and I have never seen eye to eye, and we never will. Why would he welcome me into heaven now?

Memories flooded to me, and I saw her and only her.

'Merlin, promise me something.' Morgana's voice was soft as she spoke to me. I held her delicate frame in my arms as we laid in the grassy fields in a clearing outside of the castle walls. The breeze rustled the leaves in the trees and gently blew her golden locks in her face that I softly brushed away with my fingers.
'Anything you wish princess.' I replied to her and kissed the top of her head while she played with the Amethyst that hung around my neck.

'Promise me that no matter what you will always come back to me. In every life. Come back to me.'

I chuckled at her words that she had me promise so many times before, 'you know I will.'

'Promise me Merlin.' Her voice was sad. She leaned up and looked down at me. The Autumn sun giving her a glow that radiated making her look like the angel that she was.

I cupped her cheek, leaned up slightly and kissed her lips deeply and tenderly. Pulling away to look back into her eyes I gave her a warm smile, 'I will always come back to you princess. In this life and the next we share together. Nothing will ever keep me from you. I love you Morgana.'

Where Darkness Meets Light: The Return of Merlin

Book 4

By: A.P. Whitfield

Chapter 1

Darkness. Cold and empty darkness pulled me deeper and deeper into what I could only imagine was hell. Then it paused and I felt a warmth wash over me. A soft glow came into my mind. It felt familiar to me, but I could not register as to why as the darkness kept pulling me under. The feeling of someone grabbing my hand in my vision state I looked up to see a young curly blonde male. His eyes looked familiar to me. A serious blue gaze that seemed to match my own.

'It is not your time to go father.'

'Noah?'

'Yes.'

'Why do you look older?'

'I am showing you how I used to look in a life that I once lived that was cut short.'

'I see.'

'Now come with me father. Mother is waiting for you to wake up.'

The pull out of the darkness felt draining. My head was throbbing, and my body was sore and weak. I blinked my eyes open working my vision back into focus. I shifted in the bed wincing at the pain that lingered over me.

"He's waking up." I heard Argon say.

"Merlin?" Clara whispered my name and took my hand in hers. "Please say something."

"Clara…" My voice was raspy and weak, matching how I felt.

"Thank Neptune." Citrine said from somewhere in the room.

"Is he going to be, okay?" Agate questioned. It seemed he was able to be saved as well and I was thankful for that.

I worked to try and sit up, but Clara's hands gently laid me back down on the bed. "No, you shouldn't try to sit up. You are still not well."

"Where is Noah?" I looked at her tear-stained face and my heart dropped at the look of pain that she was in. "Is he okay?"

She gave me a nod, "yes. He amazes me every day. He is with Wesley."

"Good… is Sebastian, okay?"

"Yes. Everyone is safe."

I went silent for a moment and closed my eyes feeling guilt wash over me, "I am so sorry I messed things up. We we're so close to…"

"It is not your fault. We sealed away more than we did last time, and we will get the rest of them next time. If anyone is to blame for leaving us a man down it is Carnelian for betraying us." Argon argued.

His words brought some comfort, but it didn't stop guilty tears from escaping me. Areses words still replayed in my head, and I felt like I could still feel him on me. I shuddered a painful shudder under the covers of my bed. "I am still sorry. I lost my nerve and that cost us to fall behind."

"Merlin, listen to me. It was not your fault okay? I am just thankful Noah was able to save you. I do not know how he did it, but he did." Clara brought my hand to her lips and kissed the palm of it. "That is twice you have given me a scare… this one was worse though. I felt your life fading and your body was not even doing the regeneration. You stopped breathing completely. You basically died."

"I am sorry Clara. I did not…" I swallowed hard and gently cleared away the tears falling from her eyes. "Please do not cry. I am alive. I am here."

"But you almost weren't. If you would have died…"

"Clara…"

"You promised…"

"I know…"

She rested her head on my chest and sobbed into it. I wrapped my arms around her and held her to me. I looked over at Citrine wrapped in Callen's arms. I arched my brow at the two, "thank you both for getting me out of there. Now did I miss something else while I was out?"

"I'll be waiting under the crying tree."

06/27/1959 – Until Eternity

James Hilburn Smith

July 6, 1939 ~ May 5, 2019

Made in the USA
Columbia, SC
14 October 2022

69310404R00076